MAINELY DRIFTWOOD

SELECTED WRITING

BY

THE *MAINELY DRIFTWOOD*

WRITERS GROUP

2004

© Copyright 2004
Donna Simmons, Betty Ford, Mildred Schmalz,
Ludmila Hoffman, Myrt Moreton, Frances Sullivan and Brenda Reimels

All rights reserved. No part of this publication may be reproduced, stored in a retrieval system, or transmitted, in any form or by any means, electronic, mechanical, photocopying, recording, or otherwise, without the written prior permission of the author.

Note for Librarians: a cataloguing record for this book that includes Dewey Decimal Classification and US Library of Congress numbers is available from the Library and Archives of Canada. The complete cataloguing record can be obtained from their online database at:
www.collectionscanada.ca/amicus/index-e.html
ISBN 1-4120-4035-3
Printed in Victoria, BC, Canada

TRAFFORD

Offices in Canada, USA, Ireland, UK and Spain
This book was published *on-demand* in cooperation with Trafford Publishing. On-demand publishing is a unique process and service of making a book available for retail sale to the public taking advantage of on-demand manufacturing and Internet marketing. On-demand publishing includes promotions, retail sales, manufacturing, order fulfilment, accounting and collecting royalties on behalf of the author.

Book sales for North America and international:
Trafford Publishing, 6E–2333 Government St.,
Victoria, BC v8t 4p4 CANADA
phone 250 383 6864 (toll-free 1 888 232 4444)
fax 250 383 6804; email to orders@trafford.com

Book sales in Europe:
Trafford Publishing (UK) Ltd., Enterprise House, Wistaston Road Business Centre, Wistaston Road, Crewe, Cheshire cw2 7rp UNITED KINGDOM
phone 01270 251 396 (local rate 0845 230 9601)
facsimile 01270 254 983; orders.uk@trafford.com

Order online at:
www.trafford.com/robots/04-1842.html

10 9 8 7 6 5 4

As driftwood is cast upon the water and travels at the whim of tides and storms, so "Mainely Driftwood" writer's group has come together from diverse backgrounds to publish this anthology.

Different styles and forms of writing represent the members and their own travels through life's storms and ever-changing tides.

Coastal Maine - 2004

TABLE OF CONTENTS

BETTY FORD — 1
    Jet Stream – A Pantoum Poem — 2
    Mother's Box — 4
    Mother's Day – Tanka Poem — 5
    Strolling thru the Seasons – Haiku Poems — 6

MILA HOFFMAN — 11
    Writing That Heals — 12
    Broccoli Is Not Enough — 16
    The Shadows We Cast — 19
    Second Chance – Or Last Chance? — 22
    Today — 26
    Simple Pleasure — 30

MYRT MORETON — 31
    Let's Clean Up The Act — 32
    Eureka, I Have Found Him! I Think! — 34
    Lobsters Tales (Or Tails) — 36
    Roses For A Mother — 38
        Blooming Through The Years
    Utopia? — 40

BRENDA REIMELS — 43
    Recipe For A Wedding — 44
    The Tonsillectomy — 46
    All Put Together — 53
    Collectible Memories — 56
    The Telling Purse — 59
    Unexpected Memories — 61

TABLE OF CONTENTS

MILDRED SCHMALZ — 65
    A Rose is a Rose — 66
    Melted Past — 68
    The Crutches — 69
    Winter In Miami Florida — 71
    Not Today — 73
    Rain — 74
    Limo Driver — 75
    Breeze — 77
    Squirrely — 78

DONNA SIMMONS — 83
    Forest Trail — 84
    Homeless — 85
    Orange Sherbet — 90
    Memories of Rob — 94
    Sex and Song Titles — 96
    Waiting For The Rag Man — 98

FRANCES SULLIVAN — 103
    Winter Chill, 2003 — 104
    A Change of Heart — 105
    Pack Goats - Haiku — 110
    Kismet — 111
    Summer Haiku — 115
    Forgivable Sin — 116
    Magnolia - Haiku — 121
    One Chance — 122

Nubble Light – York, Maine – 2003

Betty Ford

Betty Ford has degrees from the University of New Hampshire and Yale University School of Nursing. Her technical work has been published professionally.

She has a lifelong love of poetry and prose, nurtured from the flowing works written by her grandmother. Betty joined Mainely Driftwood five years ago upon her retirement. Since then she's focused on Haiku and other forms of poetry, and the occasional short story. She looks forward to the publication of a selection of her work.

Betty lives in Cape Neddick, Maine with her cat, Mariah.

JET STREAM
A Pantoum Poem

I watch a jet fly overhead
Travel to distant lands is interesting
To see England again is my wish
Fog and rain dull the daylight

Travel to distant lands is interesting
Sun and flowers brighten the mood
Fog and rain dull the daylight
Quiet time to read and reflect

Sun and flowers brighten the mood
Life is about saying goodbye
Quiet time to read and reflect
Others have traveled the same road

Betty Ford

Life is about saying goodbye
There is loneliness in saying hello and goodbye
Others have traveled the same road
How I long for sunshine now

There is loneliness in saying hello and goodbye
Opportunities given and taken away
How I long for sunshine now
I'm ready for spring's arrival

The promise of spring brings hope
To see England is my wish
The flowers at royal palaces delight
I watch a jet fly overhead

MOTHER'S BOX

I first saw the box during a visit to my mother several months after my father's death. As I walked down the heavily carpeted hallway toward her room I heard her crooning, *"Louise"*, a song popular in the 1920's. Stepping toward her bedroom door I saw her cap of white hair as she bent over something. It was a cigar box covered with decoupage. Keeping out of sight, I watched as she slowly removed articles. The first was a dried flower wrapped in tissue paper – a corsage from the past. I wondered who had given it to her. Then she withdrew a yellowed program and her expression showed her deep in dreaminess that I was reluctant to disturb. Next came an athletic letter and as she took it out she raised it to her cheek then kissed it. Who had given this letter to mother? I knew that my father had not participated in sports in school so whom was she remembering?

Mother gently laid the articles on her bedspread and continued to explore the contents of the box. She sighed occasionally when she lifted out an article. As she opened a small jewelry case there was the flash of green brilliance. Carefully taking a ring out she slipped it onto her finger and stood admiring it as she slowly turned her hand so that the morning rays of sunlight caught the facets of the stone.

I stood in silence, out of my mother's sight. Oh, how I wanted to know more about these objects and what they meant to her but I couldn't break into her reverie.

This scene gave me a glimpse of my mother as a teen-aged girl – something that she seldom revealed in the myriad of family stories that she often told. None of her sisters ever confided in me of a long ago love of my mother – surely one of them knew some details. Now all of her sisters were dead so the only source of information would be my mother. Sadly,

Betty Ford

Alzheimer's disease had claimed her mind. The mysteries of the box and my mother's young life might now never be known.

I remembered some of the secrets of my own life that had not been told to anyone in the family. I kept them apart and savored their memory just like my mother.

Today, mother and I shared something after all.

MOTHER'S DAY
Tanka Poem

Mother's Day bouquet
Was arranged by nature's gifts
Daffodils, blossoms
Of apple and hawthorn bush
Added to green blueberries

STROLLING THRU THE SEASONS
Haiku Poems

<u>March</u>
    Golden-rimmed clouds fly
    Ducks swim in water nearby
    March shows spring is nigh

<u>Forsythia</u>
    Forsythia roots
    Preparing for the glory
    Of yellow spring blooms

<u>April</u>
    Ice crystals on leaves
    Robin seeking sun on limb
    Nature's April Fool!

<u>April Frost</u>
    White frost covers fields
    Silver frost on dark rooftops
    Winter into spring

STROLLING THRU THE SEASONS
Haiku Poems

<u>Crow Call</u>
    A misty spring day
    Black cat slinks across the lawn
    Crow caws its insults

<u>Light Rain</u>
    Overnight light rain
    Warms air gently and springtime
    At last has arrived

<u>Lilacs</u>
    Scent of lilacs bring
    Gift of spring on a foggy
    Morning on Maine coast

<u>Memorial Day Observed</u>
    Scent of lilacs, white
    And purple reminds us of
    Remembrance and loss

STROLLING THRU THE SEASONS
Haiku Poems

<u>Squadron</u>
     Ducks form squadron V
     White frost paints roadside grasses
     Pink and blue dawn breaks

<u>First Days</u>
     Red sun, sultry air
     Marks first full days of summer
     Jogger wears bright shorts

<u>Fog Blanket</u>
     Light fog blankets shore
     It's soft focus brings beauty
     To a waiting day

<u>August Days</u>
     Rain fell every day
     Fog moved onshore after that
     Soggy August days

Betty Ford

STROLLING THRU THE SEASONS
Haiku Poems

<u>Maple Trees</u>
      Luminous leaves
      Golden hued maple trees show color
      Before winter's white

<u>Herons</u>
      Submerged island holds
      Stately, statuesque herons
      Autumn visitors

<u>Moon to Sun</u>
      Full moon shines in West
      Cold November morn reflects
      Sun rising in East

<u>Yielding</u>
      Winds blow at forty
      Mother Nature's housecleaning
      Fall yields to winter

STROLLING THRU THE SEASONS
Haiku Poems

<u>Sea Smoke</u>
    Sea smoke rises from
    Frigid water...winter's come
    With glorious views

<u>January</u>
    Sunshine erasing
    The mood of gloomy, gray days
    In January

<u>Snowflakes</u>
    Snowflakes on the step
    Snowflakes on my face and hands
    Winter's kingdom comes

<u>Spring Awaits</u>
    Snow covered garden
    My mind sees roses and phlox
    Spring awaits its turn

Ludmila Hoffman

Ludmila Hoffman came to the United States from Czechoslovakia in 1951. She received her undergraduate degree from Colby College and her doctoral degree in psychology from Boston University. For close to three decades she practiced psychotherapy, was a consultant, and held a number of teaching appointments. In 1995, she and her husband, who is also a psychologist, moved from Cambridge, Massachusetts to Costa Rica where they operated a B & B. In 1997, they returned to the United States and settled in their summer home on the coast of Maine. Ludmila continues the part-time practice of psychotherapy and is actively engaged in many community projects. Although Ludmila had published professional papers and a book, it is only recently that she has begun to delve into writing fiction. The articles included in Mainely Driftwood have been previously published in a local newspaper. They reflect her continuing interest in human relationships and her commitment to the pursuit of world peace.

WRITING THAT HEALS

Lisa sat at her desk and looked aimlessly at the clutter of greeting cards, magazines, unopened mail. Her presence reflected the dampness of the cold, winter day. The gray, stretched out cardigan she wore hung low on her slumped shoulders; her face was drawn and pale. Lisa sighed, opened a desk drawer and picked up a notebook she used as her journal. She opened the book and then, as if having run out of energy, sat motionless staring at the page. Another deep sigh escaped her before she began writing:

Tomorrow it will be a whole month since Mom passed away. It is difficult to comprehend that she is gone. I have felt tired or numb - on automatic... haven't even had the energy (or courage?) to write in the journal. Everything around me seems two dimensional without Mom. I feel alone and undefined -- as if a thick fog wrapped around me is separating me from everything and everyone else. Sometimes I think that I hear her voice or smell her perfume. I want her back. I want her to make my life real again. I want to pick up the phone and say, "Mommy, I need you!"

Tears obliterated Lisa's view of the page. She reached into the pocket of her jeans for a tissue and wiped her eyes before continuing.

I haven't called her Mommy in long time. When I was a child I called her by that name all the time. But as a grown-up, I mostly called her Mom -- it seemed to fit someone who was separate and different, but still there for me, someone who listened, solved problems, advised, joked -- someone who could be useful or just as easily taken for granted. Sometimes her name was "ma or "mother" -- that was a name for the part of her that was judgmental, opinionated, insensitive, or ignorant and exasperating. "Mom" was reserved only for part of her who was loving, affectionate, understanding, and tender with my feelings. Now, all of them are gone -- I feel left in a vacuum.

Lisa stopped writing and leaned back in her chair, aware that she was finally beginning to let her grief and sorrow surface. When Lisa returned to her journal, she wrote rapidly, letting words give form to the flow of her experience and letting only an occasional sigh or a sob interrupt her.

Over many years of her adult life, Lisa kept a journal. She wrote in it sporadically -- sometimes not for weeks or months -- but especially at times of personal turmoil, Lisa journaled on a daily basis. Lisa is one of the many journal keepers who intuitively know that the process of expressing their sadness, grief, and confusion in a personal journal has a healing effect.

An inveterate journal keeper, R. D. Heart, following her divorce, said: "Writing helped me map the grief journey. Not even with close friends did I share all the pain I felt from so much loss and internal erosion; I reserved the litanies of loneliness for my journal. What's good about it is that I released some of the suffering through words ... that I broke my silence." At another time, bemoaning a hiatus in her writing, she said: "I grieve the distance that separates me from my soul." Indeed, writing in an unselfconscious flow of thoughts and feelings does connect us to our inner core, to our soul; it releases tensions and opens us to new possibilities.

* * *

For many centuries journaling of one's thoughts and deep feelings offered those who use this medium a sense of release, personal discovery, and other deep, psychologically beneficial effects. But it was not until the 1970's that Dr. Pennebaker, a psychologist, using journaling as a tool in his research, discovered and later substantiated an additional benefit of writing. He found that limited periods of writing about one's traumas or any unfinished painful events have dramatically beneficial effects on one's physical health. Dr. Pennebaker for example found that college students who wrote twenty minutes a day about their past or present traumas, "experienced significant health benefits for six months following the week-long writing experience."

Just by putting upsetting experiences into words and so confiding inner truths, first to ourselves, we move from pain of incompletion to the relief of resolution. Even more impressive is the indication that, by confiding our pains and fears in writing, we can actually reverse the harm to our body/mind caused by prior lack of such expression.

It is well to underscore, however, that the writing process is not always a relaxing activity. Writing about disturbing events tends to arouse feelings and thoughts that might have been put out of consciousness and thus repressed. The repressed feelings that stay dormant can exert an insidious influence on behavior, create chronic stress and put us in harm's way. Awakening the repressed thoughts and feelings can produce a temporary discomfort. However, Pennebaker says, "Telling the story repeatedly, dealing with it from many angles, gleaning new insights -- ultimately leads to a more relaxed state of mind." At the same time this process integrates thoughts and feelings, accelerates coping ability and deepens our self-knowledge. Pennebaker further indicates that although writing about traumatic experiences is a particularly powerful approach to health, journaling about any losses or emotions relevant to one's current life can provide feelings of release, relief, and general health.

* * *

It was late in the evening and Lisa thought that perhaps today she was too tired to write an entry in her journal. It would be easier to take a long shower and slip into bed. But after a tempting act of avoidance, Lisa decided to persevere. She picked up her pen. Today she was aware that it was a full week since she had resumed using the journal on a daily basis. She also was aware that dread of facing the feelings of loss and grief was no longer weighing on her quite as heavily as just a week before. She felt taller, more vital and her new haircut exposed the gentle curve of her long neck. Lisa opened the journal to the previous day's entry, read the last paragraph and thought, "I sound as if I'm still running a marathon." For a while she sat thinking about the journey of feelings she had traveled since her loss, about the people that had been reaching out to her, about the many events of her daily life, and then began writing:

OK -- so my life goes on. I still feel like I'm running up a hill, tired worn out. The sorrow of losing Mom is still there, and will continue, but it is no longer a boulder around my neck. I still feel like a lost orphan, but I also feel the sense of my strength and potential. I have indulged myself in feelings of helplessness and rivers of tears, but I also know it is a way that I honor myself, that I prepare myself for being able to face life and share myself with others in my life. In writing about my grief I feel that I confirm myself -- I am beginning to get my bearings; beginning to have glimpses of life without Mom (and Mommy and Ma). I know also that I will always feel her presence, feel her love, and the love that I have for her...

A telephone ring interrupted Lisa's thought; she paused for a moment, indecisive about whether to pick up the receiver. But for the first time in weeks she wanted to talk, really talk, to a friend. She checked her caller ID, picked up the phone, and said, "Hello ... Sally...."

BROCCOLI IS NOT ENOUGH

Today's media seem addicted to reporting on the subjects of health, longevity, and ways of achieving them. The cacophony of pronouncements seems overwhelming: "Eat broccoli! Exercise! Eat less! Meditate...!" The suggestions multiply exponentially, our confusion grows accordingly, and we are left with the formidable task of selecting options that we have at least some possibility of actualizing.

So I take my vitamins, I exercise, and I eat broccoli. But it is the experience of relationships that I find most healing, meaningful, satisfying, and not necessarily stress free.

A few days ago my husband and I returned from a two-week trip to Los Angeles, California where we baby-sat our granddaughter. As lovable, brilliant and endlessly fascinating as she is, she also is approaching the age of two. And when she finds the limits set for her as disagreeable, she does not give up her own preference too easily. The lovable creature explodes with unrecognizable energy that challenges our patience, perseverance, creativity, and all the muscles in our backs. Though, in a minute she can change her mood, her smile, her charm; or an inadvertent, innocent comment turn the experiences into joy, laughter and amusement.

One afternoon during our baby-sitting visit, we decided to take our granddaughter to a nearby park (which actually is an oxymoron because in terms of travel time nothing in LA is nearby). Against our better judgment, we decided to include the family dog. This dog is a good natured, lovable creature, but as anyone who has had a Siberian Husky will attest, it is an animal who when attached to a leash immediately lapses into hallucinating herself as a pack dog pulling the weight of a fully loaded sled. On the other end of the leash my husband, whose command, "Heel! Heel!" seemed to be absorbed by the hallucinatory faraway Siberian winds, was not a part of the dog's reality.

Ludmila Hoffman

Hope Rebecca and friend-- 2000

We did arrive safely at our destination and I suggested we take at least a half hour rapid walk around the park so as to exhaust the dog and allow a more peaceful time for us while our granddaughter explored the playground area. I failed to take into account that even a mature husky tires at a slower pace than two aging grandparents. At the conclusion of the walk, while the dog was still pulling and choking and ignoring all of my husband's commands, I decided it was time for my granddaughter and me to explore the slides and other playground pleasures.

But when we returned to the swing sets for the third or fourth time, my fearless grandchild insisted on standing in the precarious and dangerous path of the other swings. I tried to remove her, but in a typical two-year-old fashion, happily unconcerned about any safety hazards or my fatigue, she wanted to be in charge and made her opinions loudly known. I decided it was time to go home. She decided, "No!" Summoning all our creativity and patience, while carrying a crying child, and managing the relentless energy of the dog, we did somehow make our way back to the car. Exhausted, but relieved, my husband buckled our granddaughter into her car seat and said, "Life is sometimes so very difficult, isn't it?" She looked at him, smiled, and with emphasis declared, "No!" We burst out laughing. The outing was a success.

Satisfying human relationships can be the most healing medication of all. No amount of exercise, meditation, massage, stress reduction, or broccoli is an adequate substitute for love and affection for promoting health. Cloe Madanes

Ludmila Hoffman

THE SHADOWS WE CAST
(written after the Afghanistan war and
before the war on Iraq)

A great nation is like a great man..
He thinks of his enemy
as the shadow that he himself casts.
                          Lao Te Ching

On a bright, late summer day when nature's bounties and our extravagances colored our future green, we felt free from danger. Propelled by busy lives, unfinished tasks and dressed in blinders, we felt safely insulated.

On that calm day's beginning who could have predicted that our lives would take a sharp turn into a dark, unexplored territory? Shock, disbelief, then fire, fear, and death pulled at the threads of our inertia and shifted our visions into new directions. It was 9/11, 2001.

So it was on 9/12, 2001, as nature persevered in her summer mood, that my surgeon called and said, "... your biopsy came back positive." I said, "Thank you", hung up and sat quietly, frozen to my seat, wondering why I said "thank you." It seemed to take a long time before the message began to wake me from the stupor and then I thought, 'My mind is playing tricks on me -- maybe the happenings of the previous day have set me into catastrophic thinking.' I moved my stiffened body and thought, "Soon I'll wake and tell my husband, I had a terrible nightmare!" But the dark message of "your biopsy came back positive" persevered, repeating like a broken LP record. The air seemed to have turned thick and still. My body felt heavy as I got up and walked out on the deck to see whether the world out there still existed. The yard was calm. Untouched by the day's events, the birds were singing, flowers were blooming their late summer colors and inviting the butterflies to dance.

Since that grievous month of September, the nation woke from its slumber and waged a war. We bombed and sent the world a message. Did they get it? We have aroused the fear of our power, though the threat of terrorism against us still remains. Our lives became more cautious, more laborious, but overall our habits have not changed. The end of war is not in sight and our coffers are much lighter. Are they getting the message? Are we?

Since that summer day in September, I also have waged a war. The chemo and radiation bombed the invaders. Aggressive treatment sends a strong message. The collateral damage takes its toll. But weakened and hurting, my body is still driven to survive. The spirit of love nurtures that survival and provides a buttress for its existence. The battle appears to have been won, although the long-term effects of the war are never clear. Were my weapons wisely chosen? Were the proper messages sent? Were my intended messages received?

Now that the dark days of the treatment are over and the war has quieted, we mustn't stop reflecting on the causes of the September events. We must continue to examine the effects of our thought and action, to explore ways of preventing a recurrence even as we celebrate our own survival.

There are no clear guidelines for preventing a recurrence of the terrorism or cancer. This must not stop us from the imperative to refine our questions and to ask them again and again -- leaving the door open for ever new answers and new solutions. In this context I continue to review my beliefs, the premises of the patterns of my thoughts, and my habits. What blind spots do I have? What weeds must I remove from my private garden? What seeds must I add to balance my nature? I take seriously the suggestion of newspaper columnist Yarl Lechman that we all ask, "What have we been put on this earth to love?" I ask that of myself and I ask, "What or who have I not loved enough?" Walt Whitman's words play a refrain to many of my thoughts, "I know that all the men ever born are also my brothers and the women my sisters ... that the kelson of creation is love." Will I be able to remember Whitman's words even when confronting an enemy?

As a nation we also need to look with care at the assumptions we make about ourselves, at the habits, policies, and politics we have adopted and followed. We must look at the shadows we cast and on our reactions to them. Do we need to uproot some of our overgrown, old, damaging weeds and supplement our garden with new attitudes, new visions? Now should we reach out to the world full of hungry, fearful, angry people? Do we dare to adopt Walt Whitman's word of love in guiding our encounters with strangers in far away lands? Will we be willing to summon our courage, ingenuity, and wisdom to create and support a technology of peace with the same perseverance and passion that we have used in developing the technologies of war?

Once upon a time, a long time ago, heroes fought dragons with swords and fire. Now the time seems ripe to write our own tales. Can the new heroes' journey be fueled by love? Perhaps the dragons of today are but shadows that we cast -- and the new heroes need only be armed with love's light.

SECOND CHANCE -- OR LAST CHANCE?

'How long, will he continue staring at me?' she wondered. In the artificial lights of the subway station and between the movements of the other people, it was difficult to have a clear view of the stranger. But from the corner of her eye, Sandra was keeping her own watch on him. He was tall, well built, and wore a light blue shirt. To Sandra he appeared strikingly good-looking. She found his stare unnerving, and yet her annoyance was mixed with curiosity and excitement. 'Probably a high class crook --- maybe a gigolo,' thought Sandra. The boom of an oncoming train turned people's heads in the direction of the sound and Sandra took the opportunity to look at the man in the light blue shirt directly. Her earlier assessment was verified. He was an unusually attractive man.

Methodically, as if under a spell, one by one the passengers boarded the train; seats were taken. Sandra, as many others, could only find a place to stand. For a moment she lost sight of the stranger; but then, without seeing him, she felt his proximity. It was a good feeling. She looked in his direction. Their eyes met -- to her his eyes appeared to be sad and gentle; hers, she was aware, were clouded with suspicion. No words were exchanged until the train began moving. Then the stranger in the light blue shirt spoke.

"I hope you were not offended."

Interrupted by the train's sudden turn, he looked for a place to steady himself and then continued.

"I was looking with longing at the poster on the wall behind you -- it is a picture of my homeland, a place of many fond memories." He spoke with an accent. After a pause he added, "Then I saw you in the foreground and you also were a sight of beauty."

'This is where the pickup line begins,' thought Sandra.

"Thank you, I appreciate the compliment." She said and wanted to add something pleasant, something friendly. However to her own surprise, she blurted out, "But in this country it is considered rude to stare at people."

"Oh, then I did offend you."

Sandra blushed and did not answer. Her usual glibness failed her. Instead, in spite of her wish to stay close to the stranger and still a long way from her stop, she allowed herself to be pushed by the crowd toward the exit. When the car came to a stop, she followed the others to the door and out onto the platform. There she stood for a moment, disoriented, annoyed with herself. The briefcase she held suddenly seemed very heavy. Upon regaining her bearings, in her characteristically self-assured manner, she walked over to an empty bench and sat down to wait for the next train.

'Why did I accuse him? Why was I so cold? When did I become so alienating and suspicious?' Sandra felt a sudden pang of loss. She felt like crying and one of her bad headaches was creeping on.

Was it only last week, thought Sandra, that I had that long lunch with Steven? Steven, former lover, then husband, later ex-husband, then enemy, now a good friend. How easy it was to be giving him advice.

"Even at our worst," Steven was saying, "even when I hated you, you were the only woman I have ever trusted."

"Woman?" There was sarcasm in Sandra's voice. "I was the only person you ever trusted - suspicion is your disease." Sandra reached for more salad dressing and continued, "I hate to he a broken record, but if you don't change your thought habits you'll always see threats and danger around you ... and you will work yourself up to another heart attack!"

"That's not funny!"

"Oh, I don't for a moment mean it to be funny -- consider it an educated guess, a goddess warning."

Steven took a sip of his water and shook his head from side to side.

"The people, especially the women, I meet are in some race -- race to get to first place, to be the top dog, to use me and each other as pawns in some unnamed game.... It would be stupid, foolhardy to trust the pack of wolves."

"Wolves are nice people," said Sandra, smiling benevolently. She reached her hand across the table and put it over his hand. "It is your own belief that creates your reality and your assumptions are written all over you."

"Fortunately, it is only you who can read the writing," joked Steven.

"Don't kid yourself, love, you approach people, especially women -- with an attitude that's so uptight, so tense, so impenetrable -- no one ever has a chance to go beyond your impassive surface. "And surface," she added in a gentler tone, "can become rapidly boring."

Steven did not respond. He was rearranging his salad -- moving the greens from side to side. Sandra took his silence as a sign that it was OK to continue.

"Listen," she said, "why don't you write your next novel about a person like you. I'm sure you can make another bestseller out of it. This man would find a super shrink, or encounter some esoteric healer, or maybe have a near death experience, or maybe just learn how to practice imagery and meditate on changing his beliefs that cause his loneliness, stress and sickness."

Sandra stopped, cocked her head from side to side, and raised her eyebrows before she asked, "What are you thinking?"

"Not thinking, just feeling sorry for that poor, lonely, stressed out chap you say is just like me?"

"Yeah -- but listen, the story would have a happy ending because, as a reward for his change, your hero would find that people are basically kind, honest and loving. People would flock to him, and his heart would heal."

Steven was smiling with only one side of his mouth, as he did when he wanted to hear only half of what Sandra was saying.

"Where's the proof for all that psychobabble -- or is this another new fad -- another..."

"No, no, and yes, yes!" Sandra's voice reached decibels of excitement. "There are all sorts of scientific and anecdotal data -- and incontrovertible research -- that it is possible to change one's own reality, one's physical state and produce deep healing. It has been demonstrated over and over again that how we think and believe has everything to do with how we feel and how our bodies respond."

"When I'm ready, you can co-author the book. But first I'm going to finish the novel that I have been paid for."

Now, Sandra was sitting on the bench in the semi-dark subway station feeling like a fraud. It's so much easier to preach to someone else, she thought, but my heart is also insulated in a cold wrap of bad experiences, scary memories. The shades on the windows to my soul are pulled down; I feel dark and dreary. She wished for another chance to meet the man in the light blue shirt. But wishing only raised her self-doubts. Even if I should meet him, or someone like him, could I rise to the occasion? She was unsure of her courage; unsure that she was ready to be vulnerable, open to the emotions that sustain the soul's growth.

In spite of her doubt, Sandra could not resist her wishful thinking. She closed her eyes and let herself daydream about a meeting, a second chance, with the man to whom she gave a cold shoulder. A smile formed on her lips. Just then the sound of a man's voice startled her. She opened her eyes, looked up, and saw only a blue shirt.

"It was a long shot, but I decided to take a chance, return to this station and perhaps find you here..."

TODAY

Margaret looks at her watch and sighs. Time moves at a snail's pace. An old issue of People Magazine lies on her lap, but she is too distracted to read, too restless to look at the pictures. Instead, she stares mindlessly at the green, polished tiles on the floor.

"Dr. Kaplan! Dr. Kaplan!" calls out a voice on the intercom.

Margaret shifts out of her mindless state and wonders whether Dr. Kaplan is related to her college roommate of the same name; whether Dr. Kaplan is trying to finish his cup of coffee or sitting on a toilet or maybe just playing hooky in a secret hiding place. Thoughts of Dr. Kaplan dissolve as the image of her father in pain, being whisked away in a wheelchair, returns. Her body stiffens again, her eyes sting. Pangs of fear, guilt, and sadness mix with an angering sense of helplessness.

A short wiry woman in a white uniform and an air of authority enters the waiting room.

"Mr. Sanders," she announces.

Margaret looks up as if she is ready to respond to the name, but the wiry woman ignores her. A stout, sweating man, sitting close to Margaret, groans, gets up, and slowly makes his way toward the woman in the white uniform. He's wearing his house slippers. Margaret's gaze follows the man's laborious progress until he is ushered through a door. She feels a surprising sense of relief in seeing the door close behind him. But the man's body odor lingers on. She shivers. Margaret wishes for a hot shower. She longs for the steaming stream of water to wash away smells of this hospital waiting room, for the unbearable feelings of panic and sense of aloneness to evaporate.

She recalls the soothing touch of the steamy water as she stood in the shower the night before. A force, like the firm hands of mother, caressed her shoulders and her back, melted her anger, washed the tears off her face. But the words she had spoken to her father earlier that night lingered on and echoed in her mind. "I hate living here! I hate you! Drop dead!" She tried to silence the memory of angry words by putting on her favorite music and later by watching a movie on TV. Still the deep pangs of guilt persevered. It was after midnight that Margaret finally mustered courage to knock on her father's bedroom door. She knocked quietly and heard no response. It's late, he must be sleeping, she thought. Tomorrow is not long from now. Tomorrow I will apologize, we'll make up. Now, yesterday's thoughts of tomorrow felt like a dagger at her throat.

Across the room a woman coughs. Margaret looks up and catches the woman looking at her. The woman smiles. Margaret smiles back.

"Been waiting long?"

Margaret nods yes.

"You're lucky. At this early hour the place is not packed as it gets to be in the afternoon and night," offers the stranger. She is wearing a yellow, loose, housedress and her hair is disheveled. "For me, this is the second time this month -- my Robbie ... seems to be accident prone."

"Oh, will he be OK?" asks Margaret.

"Sure, a few stitches and good as new. You know how kids are; stronger than they seem. You got any?"

"No," says Margaret, amused at the thought of being a mother.

The couple that sits in a corner of the room stops whispering to each other. The room is quiet. The woman in the housedress gets up and comes over to sit beside Margaret.

"You don't seem to be sick, but you're worried, aren't you?"

Margaret looks down at her feet and does not answer.

"Who's that you're waiting on?" insists the woman.

Margaret opens her mouth to answer and is surprised by the sound of a deep sob that escapes from her. Tears explode in her eyes. The woman puts her hand on Margaret's shoulder. Margaret tries to speak again, " ... It's my ... " but sobs are stronger than her words.

"Is it your mama?" Margaret shakes her head and manages to whisper, "No, Mom died last year."

"Oh, my! Is it your dad?" Margaret nods yes.

"Heart attack ... he may not...," she manages to say before tears take over.

"Mrs. Colletti?" calls out the wiry woman's voice, "your little boy is all set. He's a brave little one." She motions the woman to follow her.

"Good luck!" says the woman and begins to walk away. Then she stops, turns around and adds, "He'll be OK! You'll see. I know these things!"

Margaret feels reassured. She waves and her eyes fill with new torrents of tears. She covers her face and leans forward. Maybe that was an angel, muses Margaret, maybe she really knows, maybe Mommy sent her down here to take care of me ... Margaret sits with her eyes closed, engulfed in her own darkness. She does not know how much time passes before she hears a new voice.

"Miss Olson!"

Margaret jumps and looks up.

"I'm Dr. Kaplan," offers the young man who's face seems kind and calm. Margaret wipes her eyes. "Your dad," begins Dr. Kaplan.

"Yes?" interrupts Margaret.

"Come," motions the doctor. As they walk he speaks again. "Your dad is quite OK and very anxious to see you. We have just brought him down from the cardiac unit. All tests are negative. Appears it was only a bad case of indigestion."

Ludmila Hoffman

Margaret turns to took at the doctor, her eyes puffy, but stiff large and strikingly blue.

"Thank you, thank you," she says.

For a moment the doctor appears to be speechless. Margaret is aware of his mouth, partially open, poised to speak, but no words follow. She feels the intensity of their eye contact. Her face feels flushed. Then she hears the doctor's voice.

"As soon as your dad's ready, you can take him home." He pauses. "Do you live far from here?" he asks.

"No, actually very close by," says Margaret. She smiles and is surprised to see Dr. Kaplan also smiling. "Well, thank you," she says again and walks to the cubicle identified as her father's. Gingerly, she opens the dividing curtain. She appears to be cautious, as if not to bother the occupant. Her father sits up. His face lights up.

"Come here, my angel. Tomorrow will be a better day."

"No, Daddy," protests Margaret, "today, today."

Dockside – Coastal Maine - 2004

SIMPLE PLEASURE
(In memory of my cat)

Soft, smooth,
velvety fur being.
You capture my attention
and beckon me
to simple pleasure
of stroking you
without measure.

The feeling of affection,
the sense of your cat presence.
The sound of your purr song
dissolves the boundaries between us
and all confines of life duration.

As you turn up the volume
on your purr love,
it speaks to me
of revelation
that neither past
nor future
need our focus of attention.

This is your gift,
the precious treasure
of a lesson in
simple pleasure.

Myrt Moreton

Myrt Moreton was born in Bermuda; her first writing experiences were between her Canadian grandmother and herself. High School ended when World War II broke out in 1939. In 1941, Myrt sailed to England, married and lived there until 1945. In 1953, she moved to Boston, then Maine, finally retiring to Florida in 1988. Myrt's prose has been published numerous times in Bermuda, Maine and Florida. She now teaches a class of aspiring writers and helps them improve their writing skills so they may also get published. She has one daughter, two grandchildren and two great granddaughters. She is enormously proud of all of them.

Mainely Driftwood

LET'S CLEAN UP THE ACT

I watched him throw the empty cigarette pack from the car window. It landed right in the middle of the patch of lawn in front of my house.

"Pig!" I muttered. "Brought up in a garbage dump, I would imagine." I picked up his trash and threw it in my rubbish container.

If there's one thing that irritates me more than almost any other, it's dumping trash where it doesn't belong, especially when it winds up in my yard. Surely it's not too much trouble to carry something in the car in which can be dumped sandwich bags, chocolate and candy wrappers, empty cigarette packs and the multitude of odd bits of paper and plastic with which we seem to surround our lives.

Roadside signs are another annoyance. Remember when the elections were almost the only news the newspapers covered. "Vote for him or her" signs were everywhere. Remember, too, when the election was over, those same "Vote for whomever" signs still littered the highways. The same applies to advertising for garage sales. I believe if I put up a sign, when the event it advertises is over, I should be responsible for removing it before it becomes shredded, rain-soaked, or wind-blown litter to trash up the countryside.

Wouldn't it be great if more people realized that trash containers were intended to hold trash? Would it help if there were more public containers set out?

Some years ago, where Manatee Avenue crosses Palma Sola Bay, the public containers were widely separated and always overflowing. Trash was scattered by every breeze. More and permanent containers were installed and emptied frequently. It worked. Now we could enjoy the beautiful drive to Anna Maria Island and it seemed there were more people using the beaches than had before.

Myrt Moreton

There is one thing that really angers me. It happens when I park in a mall or restaurant public parking lot. I pull into a spot, step out of the car right into a mess of butts; someone emptied their ashtray there. Just because it's a PUBLIC parking place is it okay to foul it up with refuse? I wonder how the dumper would feel if someone did that in their PRIVATE driveway.

"Gee, this looks like a good place to empty the ashtray," a driver might say to his companion. "Here, you dump it while I back up and turn around in this guy's driveway." I can hear the screaming now. But the homeowners do it themselves in PUBLIC parking places and think nothing of it.

We live in a tourist-oriented state. Many year-round inhabitants gain their livelihood from money spent by snowbirds and vacationers. Travelers don't want to see trash blowing all over. Florida needs to be made to look as attractive as possible to woo those almighty dollars; we could well be a poverty-ridden state without them.

Surely more and permanent trash containers could be put out and emptied frequently; people could be fined for not using them. Couldn't kids be educated to throw food and drink containers in trash receptacles rather than out of car windows?

Florida is a beautiful state. With its bountiful share of sunshine and warm weather, it does seem a pity to detract from that by scattering litter all over it.

Most Floridians keep their houses and yards in a neat and tidy condition. Why can't public areas be kept the same way? Don't people notice the litter on the roads they travel? I can assure you the tourists do. How can they miss it?

EUREKA, I HAVE FOUND HIM! I THINK!

The other day I was at the Mall in one of those shops that sell clothing, you know, the ones where the ladies' wearables are all size eight or six or under.

What was I doing there, you might well ask that question, but I had a valid reason. I was with my daughter, who doesn't wear those sizes either, and my granddaughter, who does. It was there that I found, or perhaps he found me, a young fellow, who with a little training, might well become the perfect man.

He was tall and well rounded. His dress impeccable and clean: clumsy-looking sneakers, slightly-wrinkled jeans, tight in the hips, dragging on the floor, and a checked-gingham shirt opened down about three, maybe four, buttons.

He was clean-shaven with the latest fashionable hair cut, the one where they put a shallow bowl on top of the head and shave off the hair below it, then use the clippers to form a ring around the very top where the hair is formed in tiny spikes. The finishing touch ... I'm not sure if they use gold paint or Clorox, but each spike is tipped with blond something or another.

Obviously in charge, he strode around the store keeping an eagle eye on the sales personnel and making sure that every customer was getting the attention due them. For all he was authoritative, none of his assistants although older, seemed afraid of him. That I took to be the sign of a well-run operation.

It seemed to me that with a little training, just a very little training, he could make some happy girl an ideal husband. Too bad, I thought, my daughter and granddaughter are both too old for him, besides they are already married, and my great-granddaughters, aged ten and thirteen, are not yet in the market for a husband.

Myrt Moreton

Why do you think he would be a perfect man, you might well ask. You see it was his attitude towards me that makes me feel so sure.

Tracy was trying on some of the cute, slender-sized clothing the store offers. Pat was critiquing and getting the different sizes Tracy needed. I was standing by holding some of the already-decided-to-purchase items, when my hero walked up to me.

"Would you like to try on those items, Madam," he said, indicating the garments I was holding and producing a key. "This changing room is open."

"Thank you, no," I replied. "I don't believe they would fit me. Really, I'm just holding them for my granddaughter."
But with manners like that, perhaps you can see, why I feel that, with a little more training, and although I don't even know his name, I have obviously found one who could be the perfect man.

Cape Neddick River Winter - 2003

LOBSTERS TALES (OR TAILS)

For a time, in the late 1940's and early 1950's, I was associated with the Bermuda Biological Station, affiliated with the Wood's Hole, Massachusetts Oceanographic Institute.

Scientists from around the world, especially from the United States, came to work on their experiments at the "Bio" Station. One I found most interesting was a doctor we called Dorothy, who used the Bermuda lobster, Panulirus Argus, in her investigations.

Dorothy was a dedicated worker. She was quite tall, probably in her late thirties, with dark hair, almost always hanging in her eyes, and a little stooped from bending over a microscope.

A sloppy dresser, she generally wore dark-blue, short shorts, usually with an edge of pink panties showing, and her blouse, not necessarily buttoned, tied around her waist. She cared nothing about personal appearance, time off, eating, or other scientist's projects.

Her experiments included piercing the lobster's shell, removing a small section and then covering the opening with plastic. She kept meticulous charts on each subject, studying the internal organs and keeping track of how long it took the shell to heal over. She was also interested in the habits and individuality of each lobster.

"Come see what Ernie has done," she might say to me when I arrived in the morning. Ernie was a lobster that had blue in the lobster's usual dark green coloring. He had climbed over the separating wall into the next compartment.

"See, he wants to visit with Maria. Maybe she's better company than Josephine." Josephine dwelled in the compartment on the other side of Ernie's.

"Guess what Oscar did," could be her greeting. Oscar had a red band on the end of his tail; I think he was her favorite.

Myrt Moreton

"He didn't like the crab meat I gave him last night, so he threw it over to Ricky."

She had names for all her lobsters, could tell them apart, and would pick them up ... carefully ... and talk to them as if they were puppies or kittens. How anyone could have pet lobsters was beyond my imaginings, but Dorothy certainly did. In fact, she wouldn't eat lobster and generally left the table if it was on the menu.

I never knew what she hoped to accomplish. She wouldn't talk about it. I did find out that one thing she was working on was calcification. Today, I wonder if curing or combating osteoporosis was the purpose of her investigations.

Lobster Shack - 2004

ROSES FOR A MOTHER
BLOOMING THROUGH THE YEARS

From my earliest recollection, my mother had always had gray in her hair. Of course I loved her dearly, but I didn't think she was very good-looking. She had pretty hands that she took very good care of, and a lovely smile, but she dressed in such dull colors.

I left my Bermuda home to sail across the Atlantic Ocean to England when I was eighteen. At the time, I must admit, I was more interested in the new life I was to lead than in my mother's appearance. I was to be married.

I do have one memory when I thought she was beautiful. She was wearing a pale green moire flapper dress, you know the kind, up to the knees in front, down to the heels in the back, no waist, but a shiny diamond-like buckle on the hip. The color suited my mother; her dark brown hair was shot with silver strands and her hazel eyes turned green to match her gown. Sparkling earrings, shoes dyed to match her gown, and a silver evening-bag completed the outfit. She was lovely. Her usual attire, however, was much more business-like, almost drab.

When I returned to Bermuda four years later, my mother had been ill and I was worried about her health. I was astonished to find the salt-and-pepper hair had turned into a cap of sterling silver. Mother now had no children at home to clothe and feed. Money was not so tight and she could spend a little on herself. Gone were the drab brown or navy serviceable suits I remembered from my childhood. Ma had discovered sapphire-blue and Chinese red. I couldn't get over the change. Smart pumps replaced the plain brown lace-ups; stylish bags instead of an ugly leather purse. She'd added some decent costume jewelry and the scent of Arpege. Could this be the beloved, but rather dowdy, mother who had, four years before tearfully waved me off across the ocean?

Yes! Just when I wasn't looking, Ma turned from a rather

plain, work-a-day woman into a popular, much admired lady. My father loved the change and so did my brother and I.

Dad was a shipping agent during World War II; thus due to its strategic position, Bermuda was a convoy port and a post for many servicemen of the allied nations. My mother and father welcomed these men into their home. Ma laundered their clothes, sewed on buttons, mended socks, and she and Dad taught them to play bridge. She wrote to the mothers, wives and sweethearts of "her boys." Her boys thought she was wonderful.

The year my mother reached ninety she had cataracts removed and on her birthday she was to have her photograph taken. That morning a beautiful bouquet of red roses arrived. It was a gift from one of her Royal Air Force "boys." Ma posed for her portrait with the roses in her arms.

UTOPIA?

Wouldn't you like to live in a perfect world ... a Utopia? Just think about it: no wars, no starvation, no illness. Sounds wonderful, doesn't it? Let me tell you how it might work.

Yesterday, for example, went something like this: I rose at 7:30 a.m., and dressed for the day (some power decided this was the perfect time to start the day ... he must have been insane), I drank my glass of perfectly-squeezed orange juice, ate my perfectly-cooked boiled egg, toast and marmalade while I read my perfectly-printed, nothing-but-good-news newspaper.

Nothing bad had happened: no wars, no drownings, no divorces, no hold-ups, no bankruptcies, not even a grammatical or punctation error so I could write a nasty letter to the editor. Boring? You better believe it!

I did the crossword puzzle, (perfectly, of course), and went outside to see if I could find something to occupy my time. In this perfect world, naturally, there were no weeds, the grass on the lawn was exactly one and a half inches tall, the roses were in full bloom, although it was January and they are supposed to flower in June, and the wilted blossoms had magically disappeared.

Nothing to do out here, I said to myself, maybe I'll wash the car, but I wasn't surprised to find the bird-droppings, acquired from parking under Verna's tree, had vanished overnight, the car sparkled and the inside looked freshly vacuumed. How was I to pass my time until noon when the perfect lunch would be served? I went back to my recliner to think of something, anything, I could do.

Well, I could always write Helen's assignment. I fired up the word processor. Would my broken "w" have its left leg repaired? I wouldn't find out until I printed out my essay.

I worked until noon. Spelling mistakes? Grammar and punctation errors? Not in this world, they magically correct themselves. Hmmm, Pat (Cohen) needs to live here when she does her assignments was my immediate thought. But then, Helen would miss all the fun she has correcting her articles and I wouldn't have the joy of typing her stuff to send out. So, maybe not!

I went to the kitchen, pressed the button on the microwave and seconds later, my lamb-chops, baked sweet potato and peas, were cooked perfectly, just the way I liked them. Mint jelly was on the table so I sat down and enjoyed my mid-day meal. I cleared the table and put the dishes in the dishwasher. Now what? Go to town and look for that book I was hunting before I arrived in this perfect world? I have the first and last books of a Nora Roberts Trilogy and need "Rising Tides," the middle one, before I start the series.

Yes, and I need to gas up the Dodge; it was only a quarter full yesterday. The tank's filled? No? How can that be? But the pointer's on full and it's never been wrong before. After all, this is a perfect world, isn't it?

When I arrived at the bookstore and parked, perfectly, next to the door. I went straight to the Nora Roberts' novels; "Rising Tides" was the first one I saw. I bought it and decided to return home and start reading the Trilogy. At least that would be something to do this afternoon and evening. I have to be in bed by eleven, p.m. The same jerk who decided the time to rise also decided the time to go to bed. What a nut case!

Well, what do you think of my day? A perfect world? Whose idea was this anyway? I hate it, really hate it. Every ONE is perfect, every THING is perfect. No one makes mistakes, no one wins, no one loses ... in fact, NO NOTHING AT ALL. Please give me back my IM-perfect world. Please! I'll never complain again.

Mainely Driftwood

Coastal Village – Maine 2004

Brenda Reimels

Brenda Reimels is a beautician by trade but enjoys many hobbies. Working in stained glass and gardening are in the top ten.

She has been writing since she can remember and has been published many times by targeting markets in both fiction and non-fiction. Some stories are based on her experiences as a mother and a caregiver.

She lives in Cape Neddick, Maine with her husband, Tom, and enjoys having her two grown children and a son-in-law living nearby. Having a granddaughter and gathering for family occasions are among her greatest pleasures.

RECIPE FOR A WEDDING
(prep time 12 months)
From the Mother of the bride
April 24, 1999

Ingredients:

love	gowns
bride	shoes
groom	tuxedos
family	flowers
friends	photographer
church & restaurant	transportation
invitations	honeymoon plans

Directions:

Love --The most important ingredient must be provided in equal measure by the bride and groom.

Family and friends – Must be blended carefully to provide the warmth necessary to keep the recipe from souring. The blending should begin months before the wedding is put together by mixing at parties in honor of the bride and groom.
* Mix and stir several times before the wedding to ensure proper bonding of ingredients.

Choose --A church for the uniting of the bride and groom and a restaurant where the mixture will receive the best of care.

Send -- Invitations to ingredients so they will know when and where they must get together for the final mixing.

Brenda Reimels

Just before the final mixing:

Whip frantically -- gowns, shoes, tuxedos, flowers, seating arrangements, transportation, photographer, honeymoon plans and plans for resting in the future, when the wedding is done.

Gather—all ingredients together.

Provide—Music that will inspire blending, and beverage that will keep ingredients pliable for easier mixing.

Take advantage -- of the warmth that has spread through the atmosphere to combine the ingredients.

Have on hand -- Happy faces, warm embraces, hugs and kisses and all best wishes!!

Finally:

Bask -- in the warmth of a recipe completed, knowing that the catalyst of LOVE has made the wedding recipe a success!

THE TONSILLECTOMY

Our daughter, Wendy, age twenty-two, had been plagued with chronic tonsillitis throughout her college years. She spent most of her winters taking antibiotics. It never seemed the right time to see a throat specialist, as her time at home was short and infrequent. After graduation, she worked two jobs throughout the summer and come September, she fell victim to yet, another sore throat. The doctor strongly recommended that she have her tonsils removed as they were very scarred and pitted and would always be a source of infection. With enthusiastic consent, we began to look forward to a winter free from tonsillitis. Because of her age, people warned that it could be difficult for her. They were right! I had not, however, anticipated how difficult it would also be for me.

Regardless of your child's age, the experience of sending them off to an operating room is traumatic. There was our sweet, beautiful daughter lying on a gurney, looking frightened and vulnerable. When they wheeled her out of sight into the operating room, we prayed that our faith in her surgeon was warranted.

We were relieved when the doctor approached us afterwards to tell us the operation had gone well. We were relieved it was over and were told we could see her shortly in the recovery room. When we saw her, we were shocked! She was shaking violently, her teeth were chattering as she was emerging from the after effects of the anesthesia. She reached up with her hand to hold her jaw to stop the assault on her teeth. She tried to talk to us, but between her sore throat and her chattering teeth, conversation was impossible. The symptoms lasted briefly and we were soon able to converse more normally. She expressed thirst, which to me indicated that she was going to be okay. After all, her thirst was something I could do something about. While we waited in the recovery room, the nurse had me look into her throat. I saw a large cavern where her tonsils had been and a very swollen uvula. The nurse assured me that her throat looked normal post surgically. I could only take her word for it, as I never had any experience with that sort of thing. We left the hospital within a few hours to return home where Wendy could begin her recovery in the familiar surroundings.

After she was settled in, I began to hover. My mind began to formulate a multitude of scenarios. I envisioned her vomiting, starting to bleed and choking to death in her sleep! Fearing that, I decided that sleep would be out of the question for me. My husband and I moved into the guestroom where we could be within hearing distance if we were needed. Consequently, I bounded out of bed if I so much as heard her belch!

The only time she did vomit, she took it a lot better than I did! After returning her cleaned basin to her, I stepped out of the room for a deep breath. I experienced a heart stopping fright when I returned to find a large red glob in her basin! She had dropped her raspberry Popsicle into it.

I hadn't known what to look for when I looked into her throat immediately following surgery. I did have it for a basis for comparison when two days later, I peered into a throat that could only be compared to a bat cave with a variety of materials and colors, the contents of which was anybody's guess!

I was so grateful for the medications that kept her pain under control. As gruesome as her throat looked, I couldn't begin to comprehend how horribly painful it must have felt.

I had been instructed to have her drink, drink, drink! At all times, she had from two to five glasses of liquid in front of her. The saying goes 'You can lead a horse to water, but you can't make him drink.' The saying is also true of someone with a recent tonsillectomy. A few sips here and there is the best you can hope for.

There were moments of silent rejoicing when Wendy consumed a couple of spoonfuls of sherbet or jello and I rejoiced quite openly when four days following surgery, she managed to eat a soft-boiled egg!

I work two days a week in a beauty salon. I thought that three days following her surgery she would be feeling well enough for me to feel comfortable leaving her alone. The fact was that I had great anxiety about leaving her. I gave her her medications and told her that if she needed me, she could call the shop and simply squeak into the phone and I would be home as quickly as my wheels could get me there.

As it turned out, I rained my anxiety on all of my customers and they each apologized for having their hair done!

At one point, I answered the phone and the caller hung up! At that instant I was convinced that it had been Wendy. Each of the horrible scenarios I envisioned rushed through my mind. My first instinct was to run to my car! Then I thought I should dial 911 and have an ambulance sent! I reined in my runaway emotions and dialed home. I was so relieved when Wendy answered, my knees nearly buckled! If she had been in the shower when I called, she would have been greeted by paramedics as she stepped into the hallway wrapped in a towel!

At two thirty a.m. on the fourth night following surgery, I was awakened by a croaking sound coming from Wendy's room. She was calling for me! I entered her room to find her pale and shaky. She was leaning over the ever-present basin. It had a puddle of blood in it! I fought back the wave of panic I felt and dammed up the swell of tears that threatened to burst. I knew I couldn't be of any help to anyone if I fell apart now. I went to wake her dad to tell him what was happening and to find out where the hospital sheet of post-surgical information was. I hurried to the kitchen to look for the sheet. Not being able to find it, I hurried back to our bedroom. There was my husband with his face down on the pillow. I thought he'd gone back to sleep! *How the hell could he fall back to sleep while Wendy was bleeding from her throat*! Come to find out, he was trying to concentrate to jog his memory as to where the information sheet was. A matter of seconds had passed, but they felt an eternity. I went back to the kitchen and dialed the emergency room. As soon as I replaced the receiver, the surgeon called me back. He was going to meet us at the emergency room. I hurried down the hall again, where I nearly ran down my husband as he came out of Wendy's room carrying the information sheet. It read: If bleeding occurs, call the emergency room immediately! We dressed hurriedly and began our long, seven-mile journey at 2:38 a.m.

There wasn't another car on the road. Wendy sat in the back seat with her basin on her lap. There hadn't been any current bleeding, but that didn't relieve any of our anxiety. My husband drove the car. We live in the country where there isn't a mile of straight road for the first three miles of our journey. I sat in the passenger seat and wrung my hands as we wound our way along the back road. When we reached the Main Road, I pressed the non-existent gas pedal on my side right to the floor! My husband, being in control of the gas pedal on his side maintained a reasonably safe speed.

We entered the emergency room and were greeted by a calm efficient team, ready to take over. The male nurse did the standard blood pressure. It was low, I wanted to give her some of my blood pressure which I was sure would be high. He then instituted an I.V. while I hovered on her other side, out of his way. When he put in the needle, I said "ouch"! I knew Wendy's throat was too sore for her to say it herself.

The doctor arrived wearing sweat pants; his hair was disheveled where his head had been resting in slumber before being summoned to our cause. I never saw a more welcomed man in my life! I hoped he was as awake as I was! He asked that we please wait outside. We left, but having a keen interest in medicine and it's latest technology, my curiosity prevailed. I stood outside the door where I could watch the proceedings, while my husband paced nearby, as he had paced on the night of Wendy's birth.

The doctor asked the nurse for the suctioning apparatus that would remove the offending tissue. He plunged the vacuum into Wendy's throat. The same throat that we had been so dedicated to protect from further harm and to nurture back to health. Now, here was the doctor plunging this ominous tool into her throat vacuuming away the progress we had made. My faith in him was complete. It had to be done! I watched in awe and horror. I knew Wendy would survive the ordeal when, in her weakened state, she tried to punch him for the violation. The nurse intervened and saved a disaster. After all, it wouldn't do to have an unconscious surgeon in attendance!

After the procedure was completed, the doctor assured us that is was a fairly common occurrence. Perhaps in the life of a throat surgeon, but not in my lifetime, thank God!

They checked her into the hospital for observation. She was dehydrated for which I felt totally responsible. I should have put a tube down her throat for the necessary liquid intake that I couldn't gently persuade her to consume.

We left the hospital around 4:30 a.m. to return home to sleep for the remainder of the night. As if that were a possibility! Instead, I relived the events of the evening minute by dreadful minute.

We were back at the hospital by eleven a.m. Somewhere we had gotten our wires crossed. The doctor had intended a twelve-hour stay. In our panicked state, we had heard twelve o'clock. We hovered around the room for several hours making polite conversation with Wendy's roommate. We apologized for our night invasion. Wendy had responded well to her medical administrations and was able to accompany us to wander the corridors while tethered to her I.V. bottle on wheels. As we wandered, I mused about the other patients and their families, curious as to how they had arrived here. A very elderly gentleman was confined to a wheel chair, his ancient eyes focused out the window. The lines in his face at rest. The lines that had been etched by laughter and tears, struggle and pain I wondered? Perhaps he had been a fisherman or a farmer and the lines had been so firmly set by the elements. He made me think of my own grandfather. As we approached on another pass through the corridor, our eyes met. I smiled at him and he smiled back. That smile rearranged his face, making him a real person to me, not just a curiosity. That smile gave all those wrinkles and lines a place to go. They fell into place and let me know there was a mind behind those eyes. We had touched each other through that simple gesture.

When we returned to Wendy's room, the nurse informed us that the doctor would be arriving soon and would sign discharge papers as soon as the I.V. was empty. My attention turned to the contents of the bottle. I began to count the drops, estimating how many drops it would be before we could be freed to go home.

When the doctor finally arrived, he informed us that Wendy actually had three tonsils removed! Though it is not too common, the site of this third tonsil could cause some bleeding. As the healing progresses, adhesions form that cause complications, these are most apt to occur about four days after surgery. I'm glad I didn't know that ahead of time. The anticipation would no doubt have driven me over the edge!

The next few days were pretty uneventful. Each day, Wendy was able to take more liquid and reported that she was definitely feeling better.

On the morning of the eighth day following her surgery, while enjoying my coffee and watching the birds at our feeding station, I realized I had let down my guard! It was nearly eight o'clock and Wendy hadn't made her appearance or taken her medications! I rushed down to her room and flung open her door. There she was, lying in bed firmly engrossed in a good book. She said, "Morning Mom."

Mainely Driftwood

I know that God is looking after the people I love the most. I just can't resist my need to help Him!

Cape Neddick Lobster Shack - 2004

Brenda Reimels

ALL PUT TOGETHER

Making a fashion statement requires knowledge of what's "IN." With that knowledge, I planned my outfit for work early in the morning. Two pair of earrings, a definite "IN", both gold and a gold necklace to match. A teal turtleneck, tan slacks, brown boots, and a silk swirl patterned jacket in teals, browns, and shades of blue. I felt comfortable for the half day of work and anticipated coming home early to clean up the garden debris and putter around the yard while the day was still warm.

When I arrived home the sky appeared threatening and rain was predicted for the early evening. I was in quite a hurry to get to my chores and beat the rain. I changed my tan slacks and put on a pair of black, calf length tights, which suit gardening very well. They don't bind your belly when you bend over to weed and are a wardrobe staple in today's fitness frenzy. I don't actually work out but I like to look as though I might. I didn't bother to change the turtleneck or take off the jewelry but threw on a tattered denim jacket that has been relegated to painting and yard work. Besides, the jacket hides a lot of figure flaws, especially since I don't work out. In search of comfortable shoes, I put on my chunky brown walking shoes, another fashion must in today's world. The only clean socks I could find were celery green, a definite color for the fashion conscience. Green is "IN." Since I planned on mulching the leaves on the lawn with the garden tractor, I wore my leather cowboy hat to keep the blowing debris thrown up by the tractor from getting in my hair or my eyes.

As always, I wore my stylish "granny" reading glasses on my head, much like a headband. It seems to be the only way I can keep track of them. It messes up my hair but they are readily available when needed. They were hidden under the cowboy hat anyway, so who knew? I planned on spreading

Mainely Driftwood

some fertilizer on the garden and needed them to tell one product from another. I slipped on my very fashionable reflector sunglasses for further eye protection from the blowing debris and headed for the great outdoors.

When my husband arrived home, he commented that I looked cute. I didn't want to ask what he meant by cute since his idea of sexy is a long flannel, high neck nightgown. I really should work out. With his sense of fashion, I was a little wary of my carefully chosen, serviceable outfit. What did it matter anyway? No one was going to see me.

Just about that time, our big yellow dog charged, up the driveway barking frantically at two very well dressed men in black suits and starched white shirts. They were Jehovah Witnesses, coming to deliver their message. I stood in the driveway talking to them about the meaning of life and religion as the dog sniffed their most private places and wagged his friendly tail shedding hair all over their meticulously pressed suits. I apologized for the dog's transgressions and continued our intellectual conversation. I removed my cowboy hat and revealed my fashionable granny glasses. I suddenly became aware that I was wearing two pair of glasses, one on my head and one on my nose. With four lenses protruding from my head, I had an insightful vision of a housefly.

Realizing it is rude to talk to someone when they can't see your eyes, I removed my reflector sunglasses. I was aware that my attire, although quite in fashion was perhaps an enigma to someone who didn't understand the reasons behind my thoughtfully chosen outfit. Perhaps the teal green turtleneck didn't quite coordinate with the celery green ankle socks. Perhaps it wasn't necessary to wear two pair of gold earrings and a gold necklace with a tattered, though fashionable, denim shirt. I wished my legs still sported the golden tan of summer instead of the flaky white casts created between my ankle socks and my black tights. Even my very "IN" brown walking shoes seemed to grow heavy on my feet as I noticed one of the gentlemen eyeing my outfit. I thought about explaining my attire but felt that it really wasn't necessary. Instead, I told the men that I was making a fashion statement and I believed the statement I was making was YIKES!

Perkins Cove – Ogunquit, Maine – 2004

COLLECTIBLE MEMORIES

I confess to being an avid collector of things, but my most precious collection is memories. I must also add that memories are the most easily stored collections and can be brought out on command to be enjoyed by all involved.

The latest addition to my collection was added one Mother's day. I have the great fortune to have our children living near-by and always getting together for the important times.

I awakened Mother's Day morning to freshly brewing coffee, which my husband, Tom, prepared for me. Then he waited on me hand and foot as the day progressed. The kids prepared a feast for dinner. The traditional fare is lobsters for everyone, which our son, Scott purchases and cooks for us each year. This year, steak was added to the menu. Tom served grill duty while Scott boiled the water to cook the lobsters.

Our daughter, Wendy arrived with her boyfriend, Jason to share the day and make it special for me, "The Queen for a Day."

I was allowed to observe and confer when necessary but I was not allowed to actually help out. It made me feel very special and allowed for easier memory collecting as I watched the scene unfold. Tom sought my counsel about testing the foil wrapped potatoes for tenderness before adding the steaks to the grill. I recommended that he use a skewer to stick through the top layer of foil into the potatoes to test for tenderness. The next thing I knew, he came sputtering in the door with the potatoes on a cookie sheet for support and uttered a few expletives about how he drove the skewer through all the foil tearing a hole in the bottom layer as well. It caused a flair-up as the butter dripped into the flames. I helped him by lifting the foil package so he could slip another layer of foil to contain the juices that were starting to drip off the edge of the cookie sheet onto the counter and down the cabinets. While I helped Tom get the potatoes squared away to return to the grill, Scott was busy standing over the lobsters as they came quickly to a boil. Tom was on his way out the door to return the not so tender potatoes to the grill as the frothy lobster water boiled over the top of the pot onto the stove's burner. Tom was distracted by the boil over and when he turned to watch the foam oozing down the sides of the pot, the back door hit him in the elbow, causing him to tip the cookie sheet sliding the potato package onto the deck. After a few expletives from Scott about the lobsters and a few expletives from Tom about the potatoes, Tom stood up with the potatoes once again contained safely on the cookie sheet and started toward the grill, only to be stopped short. When he stood up, his belt loop caught the handle of the door. Scott was distracted by the ruckus as I helped Tom unhook himself from the handle and the lobster pot boiled over for the second time. I was instructed to return to the living room and relax. I did as I was told.

Jason watched me as I giggled about the potato fiasco. It was too hard to explain to him what was so funny. He also couldn't understand why I laughed as I watched Scott mopping up the burner from the second boil over as the pot boiled over for the third time.

Wendy was busy preparing salad and setting the table. The rolls went into the oven. They would be done in ten minutes. That was a hypothetical calculation. When the timer went off ten minutes later, it was discovered that the oven hadn't been turned on. I suggested, from the living room, that the oven didn't need preheating if the rolls were cooked on convection versus conventional.

Ten minutes later, I was summoned to the feast. The lobsters were full and sweet, the steak, cooked to perfection. The potatoes were tender and browned. The melted butter was hot and the rolls were crisp. What a fabulous treat! All their efforts had been done just for me.

Mainely Driftwood

I hope every mother had such a memorable day. I can certainly add some fun memories to my collection.

Inlet – Coastal Maine - 2004

Brenda Reimels

THE TELLING PURSE

As a young child, I was fascinated with the contents of my mother's purse. There were toys and snacks, a lace handkerchief, diapers, medicines and makeup, a comb and a brush. It contained the treasures and necessities of life to cater to my needs.

My own first purse was carried with particular pride. It was given to me to go with my Easter outfit and was made of transparent plastic with a pink handle. It contained a lace handkerchief, a fake lipstick, and a comb and brush. I proudly skipped along on Easter Sunday flaunting my grown up status to the world. I had a purse like Mommy's!

As a teenager, I no longer showed the contents of my purse to the world. It contained my personal needs, but beyond that, it carried my secrets, my cigarettes, notes from friends, and pictures of classmates with messages on the backs referring to our escapades and memories of fun times. It was the carrying case of secrets and memories. It was mine and it was private.

As a young woman, my purse took on new responsibilities. It carried my birth control pills, appointment books, and addresses of colleagues and friends. My credit cards and receipts secured in a zippered compartment along with my checkbook. Again, it was mine and it was private.

When my husband and I had our children, my purse mirrored my childhood memories of my mother's purse. It was no longer the sentinel of my personal needs. It contained diapers, toys and snacks, Kleenex, cough syrup, a comb, and a brush. It was many years before I reclaimed my purse as my own.

When I visited my mother in the nursing home yesterday, she asked me to hand her her purse. Her Parkinson's Disease was evident as she reached into it with a trembling hand and extracted a brush. As her shaking hand pulled the brush through her thinning white hair, she spoke of the need for a purse to carry her personal belongings. The nursing home only allows patients to have the necessities of life. When Mom handed me back her purse, I noted its contents. It contained a comb, a lace handkerchief, a lipstick and a diaper. It was hers and it was private.

Footbridge at Perkins Cove - 2004

Brenda Reimels

UNEXPECTED MEMORIES

My mother came to live with us in Maine from her home in Florida in July of 1998. She was not expected to survive more than a few weeks. She had a bad heart and had been diagnosed with liver cancer. While her physical needs were many, she had a positive outlook and claimed to be ready for whatever God would send her way.

We very openly discussed death and dying and the prospects of the beyond. There was no denying that we all die but it seemed certain that Mom's end was quite near. I hired a healthcare worker named Pat, to help take care of Mom so I could continue my part time job. Pat had experience with the terminally ill and was a great support to all concerned. She and Mom developed a strong bond.

As winter approached, Mom needed a warm coat. Her Florida wardrobe was inadequate for a Maine winter. Pat brought Mom a jacket that fulfilled all the needs required. The style is referred to as a barn jacket and is well known for its warmth. The sleeves were well insulated and it buttoned high around the neck to keep out the winter chill. It had many pockets for Mom's ever-present handkerchief, her fistful of hard candy that helped with her dry mouth caused by many of her medications. A few dollars were always in the pocket in case we passed an ice cream parlor or candy shop where Mom could buy a treat. One of her greatest fears was not having enough money to pay her own way. More often, however, she treated whoever was driving her. She derived great pleasure from any outing, however brief.

Mom defied all predictions of her condition and as the holidays approached, she began to realize that she might make it through another Christmas. She enjoyed the frantic preparations of our busy household and reveled in the

Mainely Driftwood

attentions of family members when they came from Massachusetts to visit.

I wanted her to have an old fashioned Christmas like I remembered as a child. She had provided me with many memorable holiday seasons and I wanted to give back in kind. I hung the garlands and lights and placed my hundreds of accumulated decorations throughout the house as I had been doing for thirty-four years. It gave me more pleasure that year, as Mom's reactions were that of a small child. Having spent the winters in Florida for many years, she had forgotten what Christmas in New England could offer. Bundled in her jacket, heat blasting from the car's heater, we took her on outings to see the lights. She oohed and ahhed over the displays. She also enjoyed the falling snow that she could view from a cozy vantage point inside the house.

Christmas Day was a real joy for our household as Mom opened her gifts and ate the dinner and listened to the Christmas music, we could almost forget how sick she really was. She would have a twinge of pain or feel the need to lie down and her illness would become reality again.

Throughout the next six months, Mom's health had many ups and downs and on June 15,1999, she had a fatal heart attack.

As Mom's executrix, I was embroiled in taking care of details of her estate and as the new millennium drew near, I adopted a "Bah Humbug" attitude about the impending holiday season. My husband convinced me that Mom would want me to do all the normal things. Admitting he was right, I reluctantly lugged out the decorations and began the arduous task of cleaning and polishing and setting the mood for another old- fashioned Christmas. As I took out the boxes containing my Christmas village, I thought of how Mom enjoyed turning it on in the evenings the previous year. She would precede me through the dining room with her walker in front and me holding her from behind and have to stop to turn on the village lights. As I made my traditional candies, I was reminded of Mom's sweet tooth and how much she had enjoyed the fresh, home made candy. On Christmas morning, Mom's warm smile came to mind as our grown children opened their gifts. I thought about how she had enjoyed being with us the previous year. I realized that God had given me the gift of Mom in her last year. I hadn't shared a holiday with her in 25 years. Because of that last Christmas with her, she will always be with us at Christmas.

I reached in the closet to get a coat to visit our neighbors on Christmas night. There was Mom's jacket. I put it on and in the pocket was a dollar bill and a handful of hard candies and in the sleeves was a hug from Mom.

Hancock Wharf Building – York, Maine - 2004

Mainely Driftwood

Estuary on the Coast of Maine - 2004

Mildred Schmalz

Mildred Dixon Schmalz was born in Miami Florida, the sixth child of seven, where she lived until she married in World War II and moved to Chicago, Illinois. She spent the next 43 years there being a wife, homemaker, mother of two girls, now married and each with two girls of their own. Mildred was a sometime, part-time sales person and eventually owner of a women's and children's store.

In 1986, she moved with her husband, Howard, to Ogunquit, Maine and kept a life long promise to herself that upon retirement she would begin to write the world's greatest novel.

Mildred is still finding her voice and has settled into a genre she loves, suspense. To date she has completed two novels and half a dozen short stories.

Working with Mainely Driftwood Writers Group has helped her hone her craft, opened her understanding to a variety of perspectives, and introduced her to a fun group of wonderfully supportive people.

A ROSE IS A ROSE

The perfume of the roses drifted up, wrapping me, cradling me. It was June, in the gardens of Cafe Schultz on Wein Strassa. We had come here after the first time we had made love. Over the years, it had become my favorite place.

With one hand held tightly in Samuel's, I continually reached across my body with the other to caress his shoulder as we were ushered to our favorite table. He'd been gone a month that felt like years to me.

"I'll have entry into the world I've dreamed of. The world lost to me when my father..." His words trailed off and I saw the hard line that stole joy from his lips, lips that kissed so softly they made me love him with my whole heart.

"Can you never forgive?" I asked reaching for his hand which he withdrew quickly as the waitress delivered Viennese Coffee and Black Forest Cake.

"Not for losing all our money, not for killing himself and leaving me and my mother to live as a fortune-less relative, treated like domestic slaves, in my uncle's house. I was never allowed to be a part of the world I was entitled to all those years."

"Look, Samuel, all those butterflies ... there on that peach colored rose. I do so love the roses." I wasn't listening, only enjoying the warm sun and the nearness of him.

"I know, I know, you love the roses." He answered impatiently. "Will you listen, Leah?"

I turned my attention back to feast my eyes on him. As I sipped my coffee, reflected light from behind him formed a halo around his head.

This was the first time I had seen him since he returned from the trip to the United States where he'd sold our small dot-com company we had developed together over the past five years.

"I'll give you back your investment and then..."

"Give me back...?"

"Yes. It's the only fair thing to do."

"But it's yours ... ours. I gave it to you. I've given you *everything* because I love you."

"Yes, yes, so you have said, but I know you will understand."

The light began to hurt my eyes as his features become undefined, blending with the light.

He moved a sheaf of papers across the table smudging one against a crumb of the luscious, dark-chocolate frosting.

"It's all there. Just sign the papers; you can have your $150 thousand back. See, nothing has happened to it." He gave a strangled cough-laugh.

I took my napkin and began trying to remove the smudge of chocolate from the paper.

"But, the sale, the money, a fortune... it's for our future"

"Oh, just sign the papers. There's a generous annual settlement built in there for you, you'll see."

I bent my head and read, "In recognition of your past services."

"Past services ...?" I couldn't see Samuel there were so many butterflies swirling around, I felt dizzy. They seemed to be flying around inside my head. The smell of roses began to gag me.

From somewhere very distant I heard Samuel's voice saying, "And she even looks like you. I missed you so much I fell in love with some one just like you."

"Who?" My own voice, sounded far away in my ears.

"Rosenthaul's daughter. I e-mailed you."

"Daughter? E-mail ...?"

"Yes, and her family moves in the highest circles of society, the place where I've always belonged, where I'm going. She's consented to be my wife."

Samuel rose. "Just sign the papers. You'll get it all back. Nothing will be missing. I promise." He waved and walked through the door.

A dark red rose rested on the table. A Monarch butterfly hovered above it for a second. I reached my hand toward it, but it fluttered away to another rose.

MELTED PAST

MEMORY:
The good part melts away
Like ice cream on a hot day
Leaving a vague lingering taste
And unquenchable thirst.

MEMORY:
Pain filled with the loss of good times,
And remembered accumulated bad times.
Thankfully, all are veiled.

Mildred Schmalz

THE CRUTCHES

I secretly watched at the edge of the window as Mother took a slender wooden box from under the mattress, opened it, lifted out a small leather pouch, and poured the contents into her hand.

Today, as each year, she promised we would leave our hovel in this mining town in South Africa, for a better life in London, where her brother lived. She had the lowest paying jobs in the mine, a washer. She hated standing in chemically treated water that ate the skin from her feet and kept them covered with raw oozing sores.

I was born, with crippled legs, fifteen years ago. Everyone said it was because of the chemicals she and my dead father had absorbed into their bodies.

I saw the small grains, not much larger than course salt, glitter as she poured them into her hand.

My heart skipped a beat; diamonds. I knew that if the mine police had any idea, we would be shot.

All my life I had heard stories of how if someone was thought to have smuggled even the smallest diamond out, they were hunted down and shot like a dog.

Mother pored the contents back into the small leather pouch, returned it to the wooden box, and slid it under the straw filled mattress. With my stick in hand, I'd limped back to the front porch of our one room shack and pondered how she thought she would be able to get them out of the house, the town, the country.

The next day, a crippled, old man came to the house. He no longer worked in the mine but scratched a small living making wooden things for people. He showed me the new crutches my uncle had ordered. "Now you will be able to walk to the train and since money has been sent from London for your passage, your visas, and enough to pay the debt to the mining company for your housing."

That night we packed one small basket of clothing and tried on the used coats Mother had bought for herself and me. There was a pair of new, used shoes for me. Mother said she did not want her brother to be ashamed of us.

Early the next morning, Mother, carrying the basket, and I using my new crutches, walked the five tortuous miles to the train station.

I trembled as the police opened the basket and felt every seam of each garment. Repeatedly, they checked the hems of our coats, and the heels of my shoes. They seemed content that there was nothing, still they watched us carefully for three frightening hours until we were allowed to board the train.

Across the border, I said to Mother, "I was so frightened and I know of the diamonds. What have you done with them?"

She laughed and said, "Just promise me that you will never let those crutches out of your sight until you show them to your uncle in London."

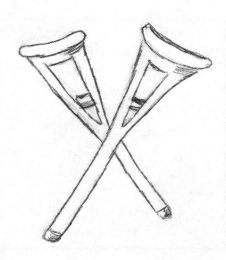

Mildred Schmalz

WINTER IN MIAMI FLORIDA

I hated having to go to the woodpile. It was a small mountain of boards, two-by-fours, planks, partial logs, a slab of corrugated tin, a tree stump or two, and other things I didn't dare to think about.

The evening was cold; I could see my breath. That was rare in Miami, Florida. Mother said there would be frost over night and that she and Father needed a fire in the fireplace to get themselves dressed in the morning. I was elected, at sundown, to get the kindling and lay the start of a fire for the next day.

I stood breathing in the rare, cold air. I imagined that it had traveled a long, long way from up north somewhere. I didn't remember ever having smelled such cold air as this before. Where did it come from I wondered in my limited third grade geography wisdom. Maybe from New York, but then I didn't think air could come from that far away. Maybe from Europe, but that must be even farther away.

Mother called in her harried, irritated voice asking if I'd gotten lost in my own backyard. I thought, "How I'd love to get lost." I shivered, I wanted to be any place but here. Here, where under the next piece of wood I picked up just might be a scorpion. I hated scorpions, I'd been stung a few times already in my short life. I knew they loved to live under a piece of old wet wood. My fingers hesitated as I lifted a piece of two-by-four. I placed it on the chopping block and, taking my hatchet, split it into kindling for the fire.

The sound of the hatchet must have satisfied Mother, I heard no more remarks about how she could send me anywhere and I'd just drift off to dreaming and forget to come back, leaving the job undone.

Mainely Driftwood

After I had about eight or ten slivers from the eighteen-inch long two-by-four I knew I would have to produce a great deal more kindling. I looked around in the fading light and found a thick limb of an old pine. It would make some "fat wood" that would burn just fine. I reached for the limb. Something slithered, stopped, and slithered again.

Even in the cold I felt sweat form under my arms and trickle down my rib cage. My first fear was the dreaded coral snake that is fast, small, and deadly. Perhaps a rattler that was just as deadly. He usually, but not always, sounded a fair warming. In the fading light I could not determine the girth, the length, nor the colors of what lay there. I stood frozen.

Our little white dog, Skip, charged up to the limb and began barking. I was unaware that he had followed me. He lunged at the moving object, snipping, and barking. Whatever was there slid under the corrugated tin slab that had at one time been the roof of the chicken run, but now we no longer raised chickens.

Mother called again from the kitchen door. "How long does it take to gather just a handful of kindling, you lazy piece of nothing? Quit playing with that dog and get your chores done."

"Yes'um", I answered.

While Skip stood guard, hackles raised, I began to whack at the pine limb. Before long I had a whole bushel of kindling. I lifted the basket and carried it to the back porch. At the back door I stooped and hugged my dog as I whispered into his ear. "Thanks old buddy."

He wagged his tail and smiled.

Mildred Schmalz

NOT TODAY

I will give no name to this day's fears.
Nameless they are fragile, having no substance.
Like vapors blown in the mist, they change shapes.

Once named they will have substance,
become real ... solid... non-dissolving.
I will not allow my fears to have defined shapes.

Let them shift and float, veiled in the mist.
Named, I will have to deal with them;
I will have to make unwanted decisions.

Today I will not. I cannot deal with the pain.
Tomorrow ... when I have prayed and thought,
I will deal with them. Then, I will name them.

RAIN

Soft, gentle, soaking rain.
After seventy-five days with no rain,
The dry ground was hard,
The thirsty grass brown.

It rained all day long.
The earth drank its fill.
The rest, dribbled from parched lips
And slid down to the ocean.

Mildred Schmalz

LIMO DRIVER

The continual honking of the horn brought the six Luchionnos to the front porch. No one could believe their eyes. There was Papa, 87, partially blind, speaking severely broken English, and driving a limo half a block long.

Let me tell you, that was no mean feat, since, in that Brooklyn neighborhood the streets are narrow, and always choked with illegally parked cars, just like in Italy.

Papa's eldest son, Tony, immediately dashed down the steps to check for dents. This made Papa rather angry.

"You think I can no drive? Wada the matter wid you?"

"Papa, why you driving?" His daughter-in-law, Sara asked.

"Two fools fight, hurt each other."

"What two fools?" Sara stood wringing her hands watching as Tony took several turns round the limo, as it stood in the middle of the street.

"Where's the driver?" Tony asked, his mouth still hanging open in astonishment.

Papa ignored him, stepped out of the car and headed up the stairs, "Bring'a de grip, like a good boy, Tony."

The four Luchionno grandchildren bombarded him with questions.

Sara poured the old man a glass of Grappa and ushered him to his favorite chair.

"How you gonna get the car back?" Tony said as he came into the room.

"You bring'a de grip? I gotta show you pictures, your cousins in Italy."

"Papa, the limo, is sitting in the middle of the street, the police..."

"Let them have it, they would'a not help when I ask."

"Where is the driver, Papa?" Tony asked again.

"Hospital." The old man took a sip of his wine savoring it with a gratified smile. "You a good woman, Sara." He lifted his glass in salute to her.

"Papa, where are the other six men who went to Italy with you?" Tony's agitation was clearly getting out of bounds.

"Home, whadda you tink?" He took another sip.

"How, Papa? How did they get home?" Tony's voice took on a pleading note.

"We order limo. Limo not come so Joe, he say call. I call on this new thing." The old man took a cell phone from his pocket. Tony looked at Sara and she at him, and the four Luchionno children stared at the old man.

"Where'd you get that?" Tony asked

"Italy, lots people have dis in Italy." The old man smiled at the astonished looks from his whole family.

"So, you called and the limo came?"

"No. Say no call on cell phone. Call on real phone."

"You, Papa, you called on the phone for the limo?" New respect was growing in Tony's voice.

"So, you called on a real phone and a limo came?"

"No find real phone, so Joe he find police, police say call on real phone."

"The police were involved?" By now Tony's alarm returned.

"Police no help, they say I call, but Joe say he call, and Mike he say he call, and Al he say he call, and then Bill and Bob they say they call, and police say shut up. Then two men come in airport and say have limo out-a-side. They start to yell because they want to know who call."

"So then, there were two drivers?"

"Two idiots. Start fight, police arrest, we go outside, get in car, I drive all guys home, I come home."

He motioned with his glass to his daughter-in-law. "You good woman, Sara, another drink?"

Mildred Schmalz

"Papa, you didn't. I can't believe that." Sara, smiled as she handed the old man another glass of Grappa.

"Mike, he see good so he tell me when light red. Al, he know streets and expressway, he tell me when to turn. I do good, maybe when police come get car, I get'a job."

BREEZE

Rain softened Winter's icy grip
Clinging in shadowy corners.
Air, sweetness on the back of my tongue.
Tastes of young grass, hyacinths, and spring,
Call me to run out, out barefooted,
Out to meet the breeze.

SQUIRRELY

When our two daughters married and moved away, my husband and I sold the house in the suburbs and lived for several years on the forty-second floor of a high-rise building in the heart of Chicago.

When retirement loomed we chose a condominium townhouse in Maine. I was happy to have a ground level place where I could plant flowers, watch the birds and be friendly to any wildlife that passed my door.

My husband was pleased there was no snow shoveling or grass cutting. A big plus for him was the association rule of NO PETS. Thus precluding any possible argument from me on that subject.

I must tell you that my husband never shared my fondness for animals. He did however, tolerate a dog and a cat when the children were young.

I, on the other hand, have always enjoyed a close rapport with "All God's Creatures Great and Small" much like Doctor Doolittle.

A week after moving in, I hung a bird feeder from the limb of a pine in front of our kitchen window. That's when I met Sam.

He strolled by, stopped, looked up at the feeder, turned, and addressed me.

"Well, something new has been added, new and green as grass--Ha!" He switched his tail saucily and ran up the tree.

"Hi, Mr. Squirrely," I said. "You look fat and cute."

"Fat? ... Cute? My name is Sam, Mr. Sam Squirrel to you. When I rip up this feeder you won't think I'm so cute." I was surprised by such rudeness since we'd only just met.

Mildred Schmalz

He waltzed along the branch that held the feeder. "Can't stand people who think they're so smart with their *squirrel-proof* feeders."

He took a small tape measure from under his right arm and proceeded to do one of those artist-type things. He held it up, extended about three inches of it and sighted along it in a line with the feeder.

"You don't think you can reach that far and get anything out of that feeder do you?" I laughingly asked.

"Haven't seen one yet, that I couldn't," he responded. I noted the sparkle in his eye and a definite sneer on his lip.

He tucked the tape measure under his arm, swished his tail, and scampered off to the next tree. From there he jumped to my roof, ran across it, then jumped to the tree at the back corner of the house. I rushed across the room and watched out the back door as he joined two of his friends who were carefully combing the newly cut grass.

I couldn't catch all the conversation but I did hear something about "... and she called me cute. Imagine! Me, Cute!" The entire troupe moved off into the woods behind the house.

Household duties occupied most of my time the next day and I didn't see Sam on Tuesday.

My husband, an early riser, startled me awake Wednesday morning by pounding on the window and shouting.

I rushed into the kitchen to see his face white with frustration. He was sputtering something about *feed* and pointing. I looked at the feeder as it swung violently back and forth. A squirrel sat underneath it munching calmly.

"So, nothing wrong with the squirrel getting what the birds drop." I told him.

"Not the birds! That blankety-blank squirrel was there swinging on the feeder gorging himself. He only jumped off when I shouted," he explained.

"Did not!" Sam replied. "I'd had my fill and was just leaving. No need to shout like that. Next time I hope you break the window and cut yourself. Would serve you right for trying to scare a *cute* little *squirrely* like me." He looked up, stopped munching, stood as tall as he could on his hind legs, and smiled. "Have a good day." He waved his tail, turned and was lost behind the tree trunk.

"Well, I don't know what to make of that attitude!" I addressed my husband.

"I'm going to the hardware store as soon as they open. They sell squirrel guards. I'll fix his clock," my husband muttered.

"Don't think so," came a faint reply through my open back door.

That was the beginning of a battle between Sam and my husband that lasted for about six months. More and different feeders were purchased and discarded.

Baffles were added, then double baffles were utilized. Finally when every approach seemed completely blocked the day came when Sam was reduced to drastic measures.

I noticed Sam sitting rather forlornly under the newest addition, a feeder on a pole with an inverted can midpoint on the pole. He had tried three approaches. At last, he climbed the nearby light pole and used his little tape measure to figure the distance.

He shook his head... disgustedly tucked the tape measure under his arm and climbed down the light pole.

"Too far for you to jump?" I teased.

"Smart-alec, aren't you? You think you know my limit, don't you?" he responded.

"Got-ya, haven't we? I laughed.

"That's what you think. I haven't tried all my tricks, yet. So, don't go patting yourself on the back quite so quickly, Cutie-Pie."

Mildred Schmalz

Now Sam knows I don't like it when he calls me 'Cutie-Pie.' I told him about that before, but he's pretty fresh and often down right rude. I walked away. I had no intention of carrying on this kind of conversation.

Two days later as we sat at breakfast I heard him calling me. "Hey, Cutie-Pie, ready? Watch this!" I couldn't quite figure where he was. He sounded far away but not as far as the back yard.

Suddenly, I saw the shadow of an object as it hurtled past the window. I thought it was a large crow in flight. Then I heard a thud and looked at the feeder. Sam, had leaped from the roof, some twenty feet above, to the rough wooden top of the feeder where he clung by his hind feet.

With one front paw he scooped up the seeds and stuffed them in his mouth. With the other paw he waved a cavalier salute to me.

"Well, Cutie-Pie, how'd you like that one?" he challenged me.

"I'll fix him," my husband sputtered.

I put my hand over his mouth. "Don't say it. Don't even think it. He'll hear and figure out a way to get around it. We'll discuss this far away from here, at the hardware store.

My husband gave me his raised eyebrow look. "He can't hear or understand us."

"You might not believe this but it's as if he talks to me."

"He what? I didn't hear anything."

"I don't really hear, I just know. I don't know how to explain. It's..." I stopped talking when I saw the way my husband was looking at me. "Just trust me, let's talk about it later," I added.

"O.K. dear, anything you say." He answered in a voice tinged with concern for my sanity.

The house was unusually quiet the rest of the day. My husband removed the feeder from the pole and made a trip to the hardware store. On his return he took the feeder and a large bag down to the basement. I heard the electric drill at one time and later I heard some hammering.

"After dark, when all good squirrels should be in bed," my husband commented, "I've installed the feeder with my newest twist."

Next morning Sam was on the roof; I had learned to recognize his footsteps. I called my husband and we rushed to the window just in time to see Sam airborne. I will vow forever that I heard him laugh as he launched himself into the air. He hit the large clear baffle my husband had installed over the top of the feeder. With a resounding thud, Sam bounce off then landed spread-eagle on the ground.

He lay quiet stunned for several moments, then gathered himself and marched unsteadily across the yard to a large pine. I heard him mutter, "She's won. I guess I'll have to run up the white flag on that one. I never should have called her Cutie-Pie. Things were just fine before I did that."

Squirrel Guard

Donna Simmons

Donna Simmons, a recent addition to the Mainely Driftwood Writers Group, is a graduate of the University of New Hampshire and McIntosh College. As an accountant and educator she's taught business English and related business courses for the last four years. While her children were young she spent seven years as an elementary school librarian where she fell in love with the written word.

Donna writes poetry and short stories and recently completed a book length memoir entitled *"A Fork in the Road"* about her son, his suicide, and her survival. She co-leads a grief and loss group in Kennebunk, is a participant in a survivor support group in Portland, and sings in her church choir.

In semi-retirement, Donna spends time with her active family including her loving daughter, Dea, son-in-law, Scott, and two grandchildren, Cody and Julie. She lives in the Massabesic forest on the edge of the rural community of Alfred, Maine where she shares her home with her husband, Bill, their dog, "Abby", and their son's cat, "Ivan the Terrible."

FOREST TRAIL
A Pantoum Poem

Sounds of a babbling brook precede the glen,
As footsteps crunch a pine needle path.
When glorious spring is reborn again,
Gone are the storms of winter's wrath.

As footsteps crunch a pine needle path,
Chipmunks scurry 'round rocks and roots.
Gone are the storms of winter's wrath;
We stroll the forest in hiking boots.

Chipmunks scurry 'round rocks and roots,
When birds are chirping a mating song.
We stroll the forest in hiking boots,
While a chorus of peepers join the throng.

When birds are chirping a mating song,
Then deer and moose come down to drink.
While a chorus of peepers join the throng,
God's blessed our forest we often think.

Then deer and moose come down to drink,
Sounds of a babbling brook precede the glen.
God's blessed our forest we often think,
When glorious spring is reborn again.

Donna Simmons

HOMELESS

Another hot day in the city. I'd give my eyeteeth to have a nice cool, air-conditioned house. That just isn't going to happen. I had a nice house once and a refrigerator full of food. Now I'm among the homeless watching pigeons in the park, lovers holding hands, the young playing tennis, and the old playing chess.

It all started seven years ago, when I met Randy. I was working on the 15th floor of the Packard building as a secretary; he was a stranger in the elevator. We got stuck between floors. It was after hours and for some reason the emergency elevator phone was also out of order. Neither of us had a working cell, but he was a resourceful sort of man and talked me out of my initial panic.

He pushed me through the emergency panel in the ceiling then lifted himself through. After prying open the door in the elevator shaft between floors 12 and 14 we managed our escape. I often wonder why they never have a 13th floor. Technically that's where we were stuck.

Our romance was hot and fast after that. He was a detective on the Philly PD, and I was head over heels in lust. I always liked the strong resourceful type, rescuing damsels in distress. He was tall, dark, and handsome and I was living a fairy tale. Within two weeks we were married at city hall. He moved me into his house up in the northeast section of town.

He wanted a family right away and convinced me to quit my job. I didn't recognize my danger until it was too late. He systematically removed all my contact with the outside world. To say he was possessive was a severe understatement. Within a year he had alienated every one of my friends. By the time I was five months pregnant I was totally dependent on Randy.

He came home one evening and found me talking to a black neighbor. He went ballistic and pushed me into the house. I didn't know why he was so upset. Then I found out. He was a controlling, domineering racist. The ensuing argument escalated into a knock down fight. Finally he accused me of screwing the neighbor and trying to pawn my black bastard off as his. Then he kicked me in the gut and left me there to bleed out my baby. His baby!

When he left I called a cab and went to a clinic. As cops often do he found out where I was. He discharged me and brought me back to the house. It was no longer my home; it was my prison, and I began to plan my escape. When the worst of the miscarriage was over I'd draw out all the money in our joint savings and disappear to some place where he couldn't find me.

Ten days later, I left the house with a worn green backpack from my school days stuffed with two sets of clothes, some personal things, and my last ten dollars. At the bank, I stared in shock as the young teller explained that my husband had closed the account two weeks before. There was no longer any money in my name. I couldn't go back; he would surely kill me this time. He had threatened death if I left the house without him. In his mind, I was his possession; death was the only way out.

That's how I ended up homeless in Portland. It's a small city in Maine 430 miles from the monster I'd married. Traveling by thumb I'd zigzagged throughout the eastern seaboard, panhandling for food and hiding in shelters, and alleys and parks when the shelters were full. If I wasn't registered anywhere I'd be safe. I needed a new identity but those things cost money. Any other way off the streets and he would surely find me.

I'd escaped three tails by private investigators. After a while it became easy to spot them. In DC, I saw Randy in a crowd at Union Station. I snuck into the ladies room and hid for eight hours. Now I spend my days watching the people in the park, constantly looking for the man who hunted me.

Donna Simmons

There's a woman with funny little hats I see in the park every day. She comes to feed the pigeons. She's an older woman and usually walks with her cane. Today she seems to have left it at home; she's carrying two brown paper bags instead of the one she usually brings with breadcrumbs for the birds. In an effort to be friendly she always says hello, but I'm afraid to reach out and often turn my head away trying to be invisible when she speaks. What if she's a private detective hired to track me down? Of course she isn't; a private detective wouldn't be disguised as an elderly woman. Would she? I can't take the chance.

She reminds me of my Aunt Lucinda, my grandfather's sister. Aunt Lu always wore funny little hats too when she came to visit. This woman, I call the hat lady, wears the same style hats always color coordinated to match her delicate lace gloves. Even in the summer heat she wears those neat little pillbox hats with netting to frame the edge.

She's seen me and is limping along the path with a smile on her face. No one ever smiles at me anymore. Most don't recognize that I'm here.

"Good morning," she said as she bent slowly to sit on the wooden park bench. "I was hoping that I would find you here today. It is a beautiful day out for early winter, isn't it?"

"It's summer, not winter," I corrected before I could control my tongue.

"I'm afraid it's always winter to me. I cannot seem to keep warmth inside my body. Ah, the vagaries of age."

"No, don't move away, I mean you no harm, my friend. Come and sit beside me, you're safe with me."

"Who sent you? Why are you here?"

"Dear, you know me. I come to feed the pigeons and get my daily share of vitamin D. Please sit down."

I hesitated then slowly sat on the opposite edge of the green bench seat pushing my pack to the side as I glanced at her wrinkled old face. She had pale blue eyes and two rosy patches of artificial color on her parchment cheeks. We sat there for a few minutes as I watched her feed the pigeons. Two boys on roller blades sped past and the pigeons scattered for the moment.

"Where do you go at night?"

"Why do you want to know?"

"I've watched you over the last few months. You're homeless aren't you?"

"I have to go," I stood and turned to walk up the hill toward State Street.

"I am not here to report you to any one. Please come back and sit. I would like to talk to you."

"No, I have to go."

"You have no place to go. Please, it hurts my neck to talk to you this way. Come back and sit."

I turned around; she was tilting her head to the left and up, with her purple gloved hand shielding her eyes from the sun. There was a knot of panic in my gut combined with the emptiness of hunger, but I came back and sat down.

"I have wanted to help you ever since I first saw you, but I didn't know if you would accept it. You always have a proud tip to your chin even as your eyes show constant fear as if you were a small animal being hunted."

"Are you running away? No, don't. That was the wrong way to start what I wanted to say."

She reached for the larger of the two brown paper bags. This one was a shopping bag with cord handles like those that come from the fancy boutiques. "This is for you, dear."

I began to look inside and saw what appeared to be several brown lunch bags with their tops neatly folded over.

"Don't open it, yet. I will not be coming back. My son is moving me to a senior apartment near his home in Largo, Florida."

Donna Simmons

I looked up into her face and saw tears welling up in her eyes. She slowly stood upright with her back to me and said, "God be with you."

I watched as she hobbled back down the path toward the stone pillars at the entrance of the park and the brick apartments beyond. For the first time in years I felt the wetness of tears on my own cheeks. I was going to miss the hat lady.

I opened the bag again. The brown lunch bags held sandwiches and cookies. One held a small container of orange juice. I began to eat the first sandwich, it was ham and Swiss cheese on brown bread with a bit of spicy mustard on one slice and what looked like butter on the other. I opened the orange juice and took a long swallow. Setting the plastic orange juice container beside me, I continued to forage through the bag. Below the food, in the base of the shopping bag was a long rectangular package gift-wrapped in purple tissue paper and tied with a pink satin ribbon. Setting the collection of lunch bags beside me on the bench I pulled out the gift. It was the size of a shoebox and moderately heavy. Slipping the ribbon off, I gently peeled back the tissue and lifted the lid. Inside were neatly bundled stacks of money, a lot of money. "Holy Mother!"

Realizing I spoke aloud, I looked around. There were a lot of people in the park, but none were watching me. I was grateful for that. I carefully rewrapped the box, placed it in the bottom of the shopping bag, and placed the lunch bags on top of it. Quickly finishing off the orange juice, I placed the container inside to redeem it later. I needed to find a private place to think, to plan. "God go with you, hat lady."

ORANGE SHERBET

I hated first dates. You never knew what you were getting into. He worked the night shift in the computer room, and I worked days. Same office, one-hour overlap. We had learned quickly the typical military routine, "Hurry up and wait." He was waiting for his shift to begin; I was waiting for mine to finish. It was 1969, at Fairchild AFB in Washington State, and the Vietnam War was the reason we were both so far away from our homes. He was quiet, but knew how to challenge you to something as unassuming as a game of Dots. Of course, I won the game. I know you're supposed to let the guy win, but I couldn't resist. I've been playing Dots since I was five.

I often came down with bronchitis as a child. The only way my mother knew to keep me quiet was to play games with me. I would lay propped up on the couch with a stack of bed pillows at my back, blankets tucked in around my legs, and a glass of orange juice on the table beside me. Mom would pick up a tablet of white lined writing paper. You know the type, for writing letters. You could pick them up four for a buck at the local five and dime. Mom always had one or two tablets lying around the house. She didn't write letters, but they were just the right size for keeping score in a game of Rummy or for setting up a game of Dots.

She would sit on the edge of the couch without a word said and begin to set up a game by marking the small graphite circles on the lines of the paper in parallel rows of dots. Once the grid of dots was set up you took turns connecting them. If your turn gave you the opportunity to connect the last side of a square you placed your initial inside to denote you had won that square and gained an extra move. The game continued until all the squares were completed. The winner was the player with the most squares. You didn't have to use your voice; you had to use your brain. Dots is a simple game of strategy. One I learned well.

So Mr. Night-shift sat down by the desk where I was marking time, pulled out a blank sheet of green bar computer paper and began marking those small graphite circles on the lines of the paper; and I began to smile. He looked up from his self-imposed task and smiled back at me. He was kind of nerdy in a way. He had light blue eyes almost hidden behind a pair of black framed, GI-issue glasses, light brown, wavy hair, and of course, the green military issue fatigues with Simmons on the stitched label above his left breast pocket.

He said not a word until after I'd won. Then, he asked me out on a date on Friday night. He'd pick me up at seven at the WAF dorm driving a red Mercury cougar. Unknown to me Harry, his night supervisor, had bated him into asking me out. He said that WAF were easy, and he bet him he couldn't go all the way on a first date. This nerdy young buck, for one reason or another, took him up on his bet, but said he had no car to use. Harry said, "Take mine; just don't wreck it."

So that's how we ended up going out on Friday night. It was thirteen miles to Spokane with nothing in between the town and the base but a long stretch of highway. We drove in near silence listening to the car radio. I suppose we were both a little nervous. I said it was a nice car; he said it belonged to his boss. I asked where we were going and he said to Spokane to find a liquor store. I asked him what he liked to drink; and he said just about anything.

When we found a liquor store, he was going for the beer in the back cooler. He asked what I wanted to drink. I told him of this neat drink I had at a party once that tasted pretty good. It was a punch made from vodka and orange sherbet. I thought there was another ingredient but I couldn't remember what it was. He stopped in front of the shelves of vodka and picked up a pint of the cheap stuff.

Mainely Driftwood

As we walked to the front of the store he asked me to pay for it. He would give me the money but he was under age and didn't want to be carded. God! I hated going out with younger guys. I had no idea from his appearance that he was younger than I was. But, we were standing in the middle of a liquor store with a six-pack of beer and a pint of vodka. I would have been embarrassed to put it all back, so I took his twenty and walked to the cashier.

We got back into the car, and I asked him how old he was. Nineteen, my God! I had just celebrated my twenty-third birthday the week before. Just two months ago I left a thirty-nine year old boyfriend to join the air force.

We found a grocery store not far away, and proceeded to the ice cream freezer. We picked up a pint of orange sherbet and he said there was a coffee cup and spoon in the car. We could put half in the cup and use the orange sherbet container for the second cup. This sounded logical to me.

We drove away from town up into the hills surrounding Spokane. I had no idea where he was taking me, but I was up for the adventure. We stopped on a road called Rim Rock Drive at a spot by the edge of a cliff. The lights of the city were magnificent below us; but I didn't want to get out of the car because I wasn't sure how close to the cliff edge we were.

Mr. Under-age said he needed to visit Mother Nature and would be right back. He suggested that I mix the vodka drink while he was gone. Okay, I could handle that. He handed me the extra cup before he left the car and I scooped some of the orange sherbet into it. Then I poured some of the vodka into each container. My eyes had adjusted to the darkness inside the car, but everything I saw as I mixed our drinks was in shades of gray.

Before long I knew I was in trouble with this drink. First of all, at the party where I had first tasted it the concoction was in a large punch bowl. The chemical reaction of the two ingredients when combined created an expanding foam of orange sherbet that quickly got way out of hand.

By the time my date returned to the car a few minutes later, there was foaming orange sherbet all over my sweater, my lap, the red carpeting, the steering wheel and the windshield. Any guy I knew in the past, including my ex, would have exploded at the mess, but not Mr. Blue-eyes. I was upset, waiting for his temper to fly. Sticky from one end to the other, I explained the obvious. The drink had expanded out of control. Then I waited for his reaction.

Mr. Cool-and-calm-under-pressure helped me dispose of the bulk of the mess; but we had nothing to wipe off the windshield. As if this was a routine procedure, he took off his left shoe and sock and wiped the orange foam from the windshield. Then he replaced his sock and shoe, turned on the engine, and took me back to the dorm. He didn't say a word.

Well, I thought, there will never be a second date with Mr. Soggy-sock. We rode in silence the full trip back to the base. I was covered with sticky orange goo, and feeling pretty embarrassed. He didn't show any sign of agitation, but he probably couldn't wait to get rid of me. After we pulled into the dorm parking lot, I began to open my door. Before I could ease myself out of the mess, he reached over and gave me a sweet, tender kiss full of sensual promise and asked if I would like to try again tomorrow night. I walked into the dorm in shell shock while Mr. Sexy-kiss headed for an all-nighter at the base car wash.

MEMORIES OF ROB

When you were born, I was afraid
you would die before I had a chance to know you.

When you were three, I was afraid
you would never be potty trained.

When you were six, I was afraid
I would never get a picture of you
without a scratch or bruise upon your sweet face.

When you were nine, I was afraid
you would always be chubby.

When you were twelve, I was afraid
you would always outsmart me.

When you were thirteen, I was afraid
I would kill you myself
after the stunts that you pulled.

When you were fifteen, I was afraid
you would blow up the house,
and you almost did!

When you were sixteen, I was afraid
I wouldn't live to see you get a driver's license;
And then I was sure I wouldn't live
because you GOT a driver's license!

Donna Simmons

When you were seventeen, I cried
when you graduated from High School;
I was sure I was loosing my baby.

When you were nineteen, I was proud
that you got your degree with honors,
even as you LOST your driver's license.

When you were twenty, you gifted me
with the excellence of your melodies.

When you were twenty-one,
you struggled through adversity,
And I was afraid some lunatic
would pick you up hitchhiking.

When you left, I was afraid
you would move far away from home,
And I would never see you again.

Later, when death came knocking,
I was afraid I would shatter
into a thousand pieces.

SEX AND SONG TITLES

When I was in high school, my friends and I were often crowded into a booth at the local diner reading through the musical selections of the tabletop jukebox. In those days, you could select three songs for a quarter. We read through song titles to pick three we all agreed were worthy of our twenty-five cents. At the time, the hits included *"I Want To Hold Your Hand"* by the Beatles, *"Chances Are"* by Johnny Mathis, and the Supremes singing *"Love child."* The Beach Boys *"Little Surfer Girl"* was popular as were hits by the Everly Brothers and Jan & Dean. The Righteous Brothers enchanted us with their number one hit, *"Unchained Melody."* But, my all time favorite then, and now, was *"Classical Gas"*, an instrumental that set me into orbit.

The owners of the diner didn't always change a lot of the songs. We soon became bored with our choices and began to search for new ways to entertain ourselves. With fries and vanilla cokes, pizza and chocolate shakes on the table between us, we spied on the boys who were, in turn, watching us through the mirror behind the counter as they spun around on red vinyl covered stools pretending not to notice our group of four. Our minds were always on boys, romance, and sex. Not that we were experienced, but with hormones racing, our focus was definitely on the forbidden. Most of the song titles reflected our generation's focus.

I'm not sure who first came up with the game, but we began to play it as a way to appear nonchalant in front of the real reason we congregated in the diner. We added a phrase to the end of each title to add new meaning to each song. Each time we spoke the revised title aloud, we flopped back on the bench in peals of laughter. This got the boys attention, which was our goal in the first place.

The phrase we added to each title was "under the sheets." Every song title in the collection turned into a sexual innuendo. We took turns reading the new titles aloud, turning pink with embarrassment and covering our braces with our hands as we shrieked.

I realized I was next and the song title G7 was my favorite. By this time, I was giggling before I could get it out. Just before I opened my mouth red-haired, freckle-faced Jimmy O'Brien sauntered in the door. Everyone else in the diner stopped speaking to see who walked in. My voice appeared overly loud in the sudden silence. "Classical Gas Under the Sheets," I announced. Everyone in the diner rotated toward my voice as I turned crimson. The rumble of escaping gas punctuated my statement from one of the spinning stools.

I could never face Jimmy after that. I would turn beet-red if he even looked in my direction. Those are my memories of sex and song titles as a teenager.

View from Cadillac Mt – Maine - 2003

WAITING FOR THE RAGMAN

"Raaaaaaags! Raaaaaaags!"

I can hear the Rag Man at the end of the street, clip clop, clip clop; but I can't see him even if I stretch my neck cause the Bond Bread truck is in the way. I hope his horse, Oscar, takes my apple today. He says Oscar doesn't eat too much when it's hot.

Maybe it's cool enough today cause Mom said I had to wear my white sweater so I won't catch a chill. I'm wearing it, but I don't like it. It covers up the pretty red and yellow flowers Mom sewed into the top of my dress. This is my favorite dress cause it's blue. When Mom was tying my sash this morning she said I have to be careful and not get it dirty. She's still trying to get the black stuff out of the green dress I wore yesterday when Mrs. Wilkinson caught me on 56th Street. Mrs. Wilkinson lives next door and she is real bossy.

The Rag Man always gives me a nickel to use at the candy store when his horse eats my apple. I'm allowed to walk to the candy store by myself cause it's just down on the corner. I can buy a lot of candy for a nickel: candy buttons on long strips of paper, red licorice sticks, red wax lips, wax bottles of soda that I can bite off the top and drink the sweet syrup, bubble gum, and candy cigarettes. I can get all six of them for a nickel from Mr. Jones, the owner. He likes me cause I don't steal from him.

Sometimes my best friend Carol Ann and I put the wax lips on our mouths and pretend we are all grown up with the candy cigarettes between our fingers. Carol Ann says I look like my mom with my orange hair and red lips when we play grown up. But, Mom says that I don't have orange hair, its auburn. Anyway, Carol Ann has black shiny hair just like her mom. We laugh when we look at each other and pretend we are big ladies.

"Hello Donna. Are you waiting for the Rag Man again?"

Donna Simmons

"Yes, Mrs. Wilkinson." She is standing by her porch rail with her glasses half way down her nose.

"You be careful that old swayback horse doesn't bite you."

"He won't. He only bites apples."

"Why don't you let the Rag Man feed him the apple?"

"Cause I want to do it myself. I'm a big girl now, I'm five years old."

"I know dear but you have to be very careful around animals."

Mrs. Wilkinson went back inside her house and I stuck my tongue out at her. She spanked me yesterday and she isn't even my mother. Then she *took* me to my mother and told her where she found me, *again*. Mom didn't even get mad at her, but she sure got mad at me. She wouldn't let me watch Howdy Doody because of what Mrs. Wilkinson did. Mrs. Wilkinson should have been the one not to watch Howdy Doody! That's my favorite TV show.

I like Princess Summer-fall-winter-spring the best. She is so beautiful with her beaded moccasins, and Indian dress. Mom says it's a buckskin dress. I don't know what buckskin means, but it has a lot of fringe and pretty beads. Buffalo Bob is nice too, but I don't like Mr. Bluster, he is always grumpy. Clarabell the clown makes me laugh, and Howdy Doody has freckles just like me.

I like the trolley tracks. Sometimes I find pennies and other shiny things stuck in the soft black stuff right next to the metal rail things. Dad says the trolley tracks are dangerous; I could get hit by a trolley playing in the middle of 56th Street. Dad says I'm not allowed off Rodman Street. But there aren't any pennies stuck in trolley tracks on Rodman Street.

And besides, I have to walk to school now and cross two busy streets just to get there. I have to stand on the curb and wait for the light to turn green. Then I have to wait for the policeman to say I can go.

Mainely Driftwood

One time I didn't wait and the policeman made me stand in the middle of the street with him while he directed traffic. He kept me right in front of him on the hot black pavement with his big hand on my shoulder. The cars and trucks were coming past us in four different directions. They came so fast my dress blew up. I got dust in my eye from a big black truck that rumbled by and it made my legs shake right through the street. I got pretty scared before he made them all stop. Then, I promised never to step off the curb again without his permission on the way to school.

"Raaaaaaags! Raaaaaaags!"

The Rag Man is riding on top of his big red wagon. I can see his black cap and red shirt with brown patches on the elbows. He has to hold up his old pants with black suspenders cause they're too big for him. Mom says he probably doesn't keep any of the clothes he has piled in the back. He fixes old clothes that nobody wants and gives them away to people who don't have much. His horse, Oscar, is shiny black with one gray eye and one brown eye. The Rag Man says that's cause he is blind in one eye, but he can still see out the other. "Hi Mr. Rag Man. I have an apple for your horse."

"Howdy there little one. I see ya do. My Osca sho does like dem apples ya give 'im. He walks faster on Rodman Street jus to get to ya door step."

"Can I feed him the apple myself?"

"Let me get down off dis wagon and see." The Rag Man always gets off his wagon real slow. Mom says I have to be patient and wait cause it takes the Rag Man a long time to get down.

The Rag Man took off his hat and wiped his wrinkled brown forehead with his sleeve. His hair always looks like gray wire. "Well there little miss, I reckon ya can feed ol' Osca. Come stand here by me. Jus put ya hand out with ya fingers flat. Thas it. Put da apple in da middle o ya hand. Thas it.

Now reach ya hand up in front of his right eye so he can see what ya brought him."

"Osca, now ya be a fine gentleman an mind ya manners."

Oscar bent his head and sniffed my hand, and then he picked up the apple with his teeth. "That was fun; he tickled my hand with his lips. Thank you Mr. Rag Man. I like feeding Oscar."

"Mornin' Mrs. Gardner." I looked behind me and Mom was on the porch watching me feed the horse.

"Good Morning."

"Does ya have any rags to spare, Mrs. Gardner?"

"No, I'm sorry; not today. I hope my daughter was not being a pest."

"No ma'am, she's always a good girl. I knows she loves animals and my Osca sho does love the attention."

"Here's ya nickel little one for dat fine red apple."

"Thank you Mr. Rag Man."

"I's be getting along now. You be a good girl fo ya mamma."

"Raaags! Raaags!" Clippity clop, clippity clop there goes Oscar and Mr. Rag Man down the street.

"Mom, when I get older can I have a horse of my own?"

"Sweetheart, we don't have room for a horse living in the city. Our house is right against our neighbors' houses; we barely have enough room for your swing in the back yard. Come on in now and have your lunch. The bread man came so I can make you a baloney sandwich and pour you a glass of milk."

Mom opened the front door and I climbed the steps to the porch.

Screeeeeeech! Bang! Screeeeeeech! "What was that? Why is everyone running down the street? Mommy, I'm scared!"

"Oh my God! Donna, you stay right here and don't leave this porch."

Mainely Driftwood

"Mom, where are you going? Why are people shouting? What's wrong with Oscar? Is he screaming?"

"I mean it Donna, don't leave this porch."

"But Mom, I can hear it. Oscar is hurt!"

Mom came back up the steps, stooped down, and wiped my face, "I know it dear; there's nothing we can do."

"Oh, Mrs. Wilkinson. Will you watch Donna? Please don't let her leave the porch!" I looked up and Mrs. Wilkinson was standing on the other side of the porch rail again with a dishtowel in her hands.

"I was just doing up my lunch dishes and I heard an awful racket. Was there an accident on 56th Street?"

"Yes, I think it was the Rag Man."

Donna on Rodman Street - 1951

Frances Sullivan

Frances Sullivan has been a nurse, watercolor artist, innkeeper, and substitute teacher. Having done much traveling with her husband, they wrote two published travel guides. The one on Irish Bed and Breakfasts is out in its fifth edition now. She has written seriously for twenty-five years, trying her hand at novels, short stories and human-interest stories for her local newspapers. Recently she was thrilled to see a short play, written from *"Forgivable Sin,"* acted on the stage of the Firehouse in Newburyport. She is most proud of being a mother of two married girls with four grandchildren.

WINTER CHILL, 2003

Nine-Eleven.

George Dubya,
Mad at Saddam.
War drums rumble.

Colombia crumbles.

North Korea, shaking fists.

Snow, ice; more snow, ice;
Rain, ice, more & more snow,
While our money - melts - away.

TV blares: "Your roof could cave in!"

I don't feel so good.

I feel *SCARED* - **sad** - and small.

Frances Sullivan

A CHANGE OF HEART

Julie had seen him so many times, in Drama Club, and standing up on the stage, debating with Daniel Shaw, who everyone knew would be a lawyer some day. His name was Jimmy Cavallo and he was fat. It had been her habit to look right through fat people. For one thing, Julie couldn't tolerate their clownish appearance. For another, she pictured them gulping down huge bowls full of cereal, plates of steak, chops and potatoes. Isn't that how Uncle Morrie got so fat? 'Course Jimmy wasn't as big as Uncle Morrie. But his chest and tummy and butt were well-padded.

Even though he didn't play sports, the other boys seemed to like him. He knew how to joke and make them laugh. The entertainer. But the girls prattled on about what a pill Jimmy was, and how his body jiggled and he moved so slowly. They said he was arrogant, a "know it all." Julie noticed he was smart, though. In Mr. Cuddire's history class, he raised his hand a lot and knew about General Lee and General Meade at Gettysburg, and how the war was really a loss for both the North and the South. He seemed to know a lot of little items that Julie had never thought about.

Then Julie's world shifted. It was November 10th, the night of the Big Dance, the first her parents allowed her to attend. They came through on their promise that she could go after her sixteenth birthday, which had been just in time, two weeks before. Julie was thrilled. She and her best friend, Tricia tried on every dress they both owned. Julie settled on an overlay of two shirts, a pale orange and a bright pink, and the gray-blue cotton jumper that hid her boobs. Tricia chose a purple mini-skirt and white angora top. She had the greatest long limbs. Julie thought the top of her own legs were too plump for mini-skirts.

Mainely Driftwood

"Oh, Jule, why not something more glamorous?" asked Tricia.

She lifted her eyebrow and shook the tops of the jumper straps. "I'm going for comfort. My first time, anyway." She sat down and leaned forward while Tricia pulled her dark hair into a French braid, leaving a few curls tucked around the ends.

As they entered the gym, Julie's heart soared as they spotted the brightly colored crepe paper loops for the Spanish Fiesta theme. A huge purple donkey piñata hung from the ceiling, and lights flickered over the walls from the spinning mirrored ball behind it. On a low platform to one side, Franklin Stover's little band played, *Spanish Eyes.*"

Julie and Tricia joined a small group of girls, standing in front of the band, chatting and laughing. They nodded and gestured towards the packs of males, who looked out of place, scratching their arms, sneaking peeks back and giggling like hyenas or bopping each other on the arms.

Shelly was the leader of Julie's herd. Julie thought she was so elegant in her blonde updo, and pale green short shift that showed off her perfect shape and runners legs. Oh God, what I wouldn't do for a bod like hers, she dreamed. The girls huddled together, clutching their little purses that held lipstick comb and perfume. Julie had her eye on a thin, shy boy at the edge of the crowd near the seating stands. She went for those droopy dark eyes. The band played a sexy number, with a drum rhythm from the Congo. First Shelly got picked, then two other girls moved out. Julie and Tricia stood alone, smiling fakely and moving their hips to the music. "Shy boy" sauntered over. Julie's heart beat like a jack-hammer and her throat felt dry. He walked awkwardly up to Tricia and led her onto the floor touching her lightly. Julie felt tears well up. She swallowed and waved at her friend.

She stood awhile, leaning on the bandstand, then relaxed and sat on the edge. I'm not going to get asked. There goes Billy Martin with Marilyn Hicks. He's cute. She tried to catch his eye and smile. Then Jimmy Cavallo swung by, with Mary Baines. Mary with the sausage curls tucked up in back. Julie's eyes stayed on the pair sailing along. Hmm, he's not a bad dancer. Wouldn't I like to float around like that? He held Mary close and looked into her face. They moved like liquid silver. A swell rose up in Julie's chest, it hurt, like jealousy and want. Can you believe it? I actually want to dance with Jimmy. Forget it. I can't be seen with him. The song ended and Tricia came scurrying back.

"This is a good place to stand," Tricia whispered. "That was Tracy Scott. Wasn't he cute? He can't dance, but oh those eyes make me melt." Julie barely heard, her eyes following Jimmy Cavallo as he stepped up to the punch bowl and ladled. He looked up and caught her eye, then he disappeared. A moment later, his voice at her side surprised her. "Hi Julie. I brought you this. You looked thirsty." He handed her a cup. She looked around, hoping no one saw.

"Thank you." She reached for the cup and saw his dark blue eyes flash, his face turn handsome with a confident smile showing off his perfect white teeth. Her heart did a flippity-flop. What the heck? She drank the punch right down and looked for a place to put the cup. Jimmy took it to a trash barrel. As he walked back toward her she noticed his neat dark dress jacket and navy tie. His longish hair was slicked back from his face. He walked as though he were content with himself, his head held high, looking around, nodding at kids.

A slow song started, *"You Can't Take that Away from Me."* Jimmy walked up to Julie and held out his arms. She couldn't turn him down. She slid right into those arms and was enveloped cozily, smelling the apple-spice cologne on his cheek. He really knew how to lead, as Julie seemed to float off the dance floor. It was heavenly. He moved to and fro, feeling the beat and tempo, swooping her around at just the right moment, leaving her a bit dizzy. She laughed and he smiled as he pulled her in so her head leaned on his broad shoulder, his silky cheek touched hers. His hand moved up to the middle of her back and down to her waist again. Julie felt complete, satisfied and dreamy. Could this be possible, with Jimmy Cavallo? His hug felt scrumptious, as she'd never had more than a fleeting one in her life.

He murmured in her ear, "I love the way your hair looks, Julie. Like a princess." She thanked him. With her hand she caressed his shoulder. Wasn't it nice to hear a compliment like that? Tricia's the only person who'd ever given her one before. One that really counted anyway. The song ended and Jimmy walked her back to her spot, and squeezed her hand as he thanked her. By the time he walked away, Julie was full of so many feelings. A swollen heart, fluttery tickles in her arms and legs, and her head was on the moon.

Alone a few minutes, she thought, Wow, he's not so bad. I wonder if he'll ask me again? Tricia returned, gabbing about her luck with lanky Tracy Scott. "Who did you dance with? I looked over and you were gone. I know you danced."

Julie took a deep breath. I danced with Jimmy Cavallo. It was great. He's a smooth dancer." She waited for the ridicule.

"Yeah, I've been watching him myself. I like the way he moves. Must have been fun, huh?"

"More than that. It was really groovy. I hope he comes back." They stood there starlit and smiling at who knows what? The next dance Jimmy swung by with Cara Simpson. Damn her, with those long auburn tresses, flipping from side to side. His eyes were on Julie, though, no matter which angle they were at. Pleased, Julie followed his attentive gaze till he was out of sight.

The last dance, another slow one, Julie searched the dance floor, filling with couples snuggling close. Tricia got snatched and she hoped she wouldn't have to sit this one out. Then Jimmy stood before her, his eyebrows raised in anticipation. She flowed into his arms, was carried off again into a trail of delight, her body held closely, rocking to Linda Ronstadt's torchy song. The syncopated drumbeat woke something inside Julie. She liked being merged with Jimmy. He was polite, clean, affectionate, although he spoke little, she knew he had a brain. A bit overwhelmed, she found her thoughts instead of "He's nice but he's fat so he's off limits" were, "So what if he's fat?" She liked the hard muscles she felt in his arms and shoulders, he smelled divine and danced wonderfully. She couldn't think why his being fat ever disturbed her.

The dance was done. "Thank you princess for a lovely evening. Would you go to the show with me some time? Maybe Saturday?"

"Sure, I'd like that," Julie answered.

The band played the *"Mexican Hat Dance"*, while the piñata was lowered. Time to take turns smacking it. As Julie took her turn she held the paddle high and smashed the poor donkey open, candy spraying everywhere. Kids scrambled to collect it. Julie laughed hard and backed up, wondering who got the paddle next. She backed right into Jimmy Cavallo's open arms. He lifted her high. "You did it. You broke the piñata, Yea!" he yelled. He turned her around. As she slid down his front and her feet touched the floor, he kissed her lightly, soft lips brushing over hers, making her insides dance. Right in front of the whole crowd.

For a fleeting second, she thought. Oh geez are they gonna laugh? Then she dismissed them entirely. Laugh away you fools. This feels too nice. They walked hand in hand to her mother's station wagon.

"See you Saturday, then?" he leaned in to say.

"Yes, I hope so." She waved goodbye.

Julie and her mom rode in silence for a few minutes.

"See you? Where?" her mom asked, shifting into third gear.

"We're going to a show. Is that all right, if Tricia goes, too?"

"With Jimmy? I guess so. But honey, he's so fat."

Julie glared at her mother's profile. "No, he isn't."

Mom lifted her chin and looked straight ahead. "Okay," she said softly.

PACK GOATS

Joe's funny pack goats
Poop like Vegas slot machines
On boards of lean-to.

Joe's Alpine pack goats
Do nightly Irish step-dance,
Keeping him awake.

Frances Sullivan

KISMET

At seven one Sunday morning, Doris got report from the night nurse. A new man had been admitted to Room 307--name of Lahey. Thomas, wasn't it? She was assigned to him. Another heart attack in the wee hours. He'd be on oxygen and several medications. She'd have to measure his intake and output and give him a bed bath. Doris decided to check on him first. He was on his side, facing the window; his oxygen hissed lightly at 2 liters. The curtains were already parted. A pink glow imbued the sky.

Walking over to the bed, she said softly, "Thomas," as her hand touched his shoulder. He rolled back to look at her. "Good morning." She fluffed up his pillow and helped him hike up in bed. Their heads became very close.

He folded an arm behind his head. Clear blue eyes studied her through glasses. A crease formed in his forehead. "Doris?" he asked. "Doris Fielding?"

How could he know my maiden name? she wondered. His face was nice-looking though pale, with those long lines in his cheeks that she liked. He looked about early 60's, hair thinning but not all gray yet. Husky but not overweight. Looked familiar, but from where?

"Tom," she said to herself "Tom Lahey?" She stepped back, her hand flying to her mouth. "Oh, my God, Tommy! It's you?" She heard a nervous laugh escape.

He wrapped his warm hand around her wrist that lay on his bed. "It is you, isn't it?" He laughed, a familiar low sexy laugh. The years peeled back for Doris. She and Tom, 30-35 years younger, lying next to each other on a cot in his tiny apartment on Beacon Hill, holding hands, gazing quietly into each others eyes.

No. Could this be the same man?

"Yes," he laughed again. "It is me, Doris. Isn't this the strangest quirk of fate? For you to be my nurse, after all these years?"

She couldn't help putting her hand on his arm, up near his shoulder.

"Oh, my goodness. It's so good to see you. I don't have to ask how..."

She saw a sheen come over his eyes. "Aw, Doris, this is my second goddamned attack. Don't figure I've got much longer now."

"Tommy, don't say that. If you take it slow and easy, you'll last along time. There are some great new heart medications now." She smiled and turned away from the billow of sympathy she felt in her gut. Straightening his water glass and newspaper on his bedside table, she asked, "Would you like a drink now? Breakfast should be in soon."

"Thanks, I would." He accepted the sip of water, held the bottom of the glass, his hand touching hers. A zing went across her belly. Their eyes held each other as they had long ago. She was still attracted to him. Why had they parted? Oh, yeah, the Peace Corps. He'd asked her to go with him to South Africa. She wasn't ready to deal with primitive Third World conditions. He'd written a few times--said he was so busy teaching natives how to plant and care for growing corn.

Oh, Jesus. She recalled how much she liked this energized, funny, totally focused man. His breakfast tray was set down by a kitchen aide. Doris rolled up the bed and pushed his table closer for him to reach it, She poured the coffee and he took a sip. "Where have you been, Tom? I can't get over seeing you back here, in New England." She smiled widely.

"I work in Philadelphia. Came home to see my mom, who's been ill."

"Do you have a family?" she asked. She lifted the metal cover on the main course. Oatmeal. Her stomach objected.

Frances Sullivan

He peered into the cereal, then lay back and sighed. "I do. Yes. I live with one of my two sons. They're great guys. One's a lawyer; one's a teacher. Been divorced twelve years now."

There was deep hurt in his eyes. "I'm sorry. Me, too. Divorced, I mean, for a long while. My four kids are all grown, of course. Want me to fix this for you?" she asked, reaching for the milk pitcher.

"No, thanks, I can manage." His eyes met hers one more time before he poured the milk onto his cereal, a half smile curving his wide flat lips. They hadn't changed in all these years. She thought of her own 60-year-old face, wrinkles here and there. Reluctantly, she said softly, "I'll let you rest now. Gotta go see my other patients. I'll be back real soon." She flicked him a wave and walked by the nurses station. As she helped a sputtering woman into her chair, Doris realized that she wished she could spend the whole morning with Tom. Did he have a girlfriend? Would she be coming in to stay with him? There were so many questions she'd like to ask. How long had he lived in Philly? What kind of work did he do?

Doris had married Peter Konos, a builder, about nine months after Tom's letters stopped. Pete had been an exciting wooer, flowers, dancing dates, the works. But once the prize was won, he became a cool companion, expecting his meals on time, perking up only when each of his four children was born. His work kept him out of the house 60 hours or more a week, leaving the whole house and childcare to Doris. They parted when their oldest was sixteen. He'd asked her to move to Virginia where building was booming. She said, "No." Bad enough to be lonely in her own home town. He commuted for a year, then stopped coming home. She knew he'd found a woman, younger and naive to his ways.

Doris heard the shower turn off just as she finished making the bed of the last of her three other patients. She checked and helped her cranky patient to dry off and get dressed. The woman's nasal complaining droned on unheard. Doris hustled her between clean sheets and turned off the light. With a small thrill in her chest she headed for Tom's room. Startled, she saw Nancy Clarke rolling the Code Cart out of his room. The paddles were unwrapped and greasy. Her heart dropped. She hadn't heard any bustle from around the corner. Doctor Quimby, scratching his beard, and another nurse appeared in Tom's doorway.

"Is he...?" Doris asked breathlessly.

The doctor reached out and touched her arm. Shit. He was gone, wasn't he? "No, no. He's okay. Had us pretty scared for a few minutes, though. Adrenalin pulled him out of it. Keep him on bed rest. I've upped his Cardizem." He showed her the new orders on Tom's chart. She wrote down the changes on her pad, fingers numb, heart still galloping. Then she walked to the window-side bed.

Tom's face was flour-white, his lips cracked. His eyelids lifted heavily. "Doris," he uttered, "I almost faded out there. Where were you?"

"I ... I was washing my other patients. Sorry, I didn't even realize... Do you want me to wash you now?" God, it sounded so intimate.

He closed his eyes and smiled. "That sounds tempting, Honey, but I'm way too tired. Could you give me a little back rub?"

She helped him turn on his side, and arranged his oxygen and IV tubing. Pushing the johnny aside, she powdered his back and began the long, firm stroking over the broad expanse of tanned silky skin, moving up and out and starting at his waist again. He felt the same under her fingers. She rubbed and rubbed, longing to lay her head on his warm back and caress it as she had so many years ago. She'd kissed his sides then.. up and up until she reached his shoulder, then she'd pressed her bare breasts into his back and felt his firm buttocks under her belly. She'd nestled her face into the curve of his shoulder and kissed him deeply into the hollow near his neck. He reached back and moved her body up and down until she took over on her own.

"Oh, God. This is him. This is Tom, my lover," she cried inside herself. What had happened to all that love? Suddenly she realized her cheek was against his back and tears plunked down on his skin.

Tom turned around and reached out his arms. She fell into them. "Am I pressing too hard?" she asked. Her cheek moved on his scratchy one, his oxygen tube hanging to one side.

"No, no, Doris," He swallowed. "I've thought of you this way so many times. So many, many times." He rubbed her back. She knew she'd probably get fired if anyone walked in but she cared not a whit.

"Tom, if.. if..."

"Shh," he said, touching his finger to her lips. "No ifs. This is all we have. This moment. Let's just feel it, and savor it. It feels so good." She nodded and let herself meld into his embrace.

SUMMER HAIKU

Sun, a yellow glow
in mist on reservoir. Geese
flirt, with honk and chase.

Ain't it nice? I push
hand mower, no smoke, smell, rumble.
Just friendly flutter.

FORGIVABLE SIN

God forgive me, there he is again. He nods to me in church and I cannot but nod back. It's only polite. When we step outside, he sometimes bumps into me in a deliciously intimate way. Just a shoulder or a hip, then he moves quickly aside and says, "Oh, pardon me." He tips his hat. "So sorry, Ma'am."

So now when it happens, I nod again and smile. He lifts his eyebrows to where he parks his auto, behind the tall fence down the road. I know what he means. Francis, my dear spouse, goes off to help count the money. He's the pastor. I know he'll be occupied with this and deacons meetings and interviews with Sunday School teachers for at least three more hours. I walk quickly past a host of parishioners. I hope they think I am walking home. It begins to sprinkle and I raise my face to enjoy the warm wetness before I snap up my little parasol.

Delkins long, sleek black auto is way down behind a hedgerow at the edge of the park. I step delicately over the wet blades of grass, dampening the hem of my taffeta skirt and I hear the car door being opened from the inside. Excitement rouses up in me as I hurry round and get in. "Good morning," he says as he lifts my gloved hand to his mouth to kiss it. I like his brown face against the white glove that's unbuttoned at the wrist. He turns over my hand and presses his soft lips on the very spot where the glove lies open, all the while gazing thoughtfully at me with those deep brown eyes. Oh, Delkins, if you only knew. I have never felt like this with Francis.

He turns on the motor and the Franklin starts, humming smoothly, unlike Francis's Ford. Delkins looks at me, his wide lips curling up as if to say, "Hear that? Isn't that a beautiful sound?"

I place my hand on his arm. The fine strength of his muscle can be felt even through the wool coat.

"This is so nice, D-Delkins. I love these rides we take." I peer through the misted window.

"Well, thank you my lady." His voice deep and mellow. "Would you call me Wendall, please?"

"Oh, yes, of course. You want me to use your proper name. You--you may call me Caroline, too. I'd like that." Wendall, the name wraps around me.

He tries the name, "Caroline" spoken in his melodious bass. The name becomes a soothing balm that bottoms into my belly.

Wendall begins to hum, a piece of a hymn the choir has just finished, *"What a Friend We Have in Jesus."* Then the words come softly, with air in them. *"Have we trials and temptations? Is there trouble anywhere? We should never be discouraged. Take it to the Lord in prayer."* He looks at me off and on while he sings and he nods, smiling. I join in at the last line of the song, *"In His arms He'll take and shield thee, thou wilt find a solace there."*

Wendall flashes a broad smile at me and winks. We often start our rides with a hymn. This is our ninth ride-out together. I remember every hymn, because I love to hear him pronounce certain words, like "precious," "bountiful," "mountains," "temptation." I don't think about the words. They are just there to pronounce and play with on our tongues.

It all started one Sunday when I was walking home from church in a downpour. The Marbles offered me a ride, but I declined. It being summer, I was sure the rain would stop. But soon I saw my new gray kid shoes were getting all muddy. The big black car pulled up alongside me, and there he was. Wendall Delkins, the master mechanic, who had pulled our Ford out of the doldrums. He cast a big smile at me and gestured towards him, rolling down the window. "Oh, yes."

"Thank you so much, Mr. Delkins," I said as I closed my umbrella and got in beside him.

"Delighted to help you out, Mrs. Miller." I closed the door.

"Oh, dear, I'm getting your nice seats all wet."

"Not a problem at all," he said, smiling again.

"I didn't see you in church," I said, tucking my hair under my hat.

"Oh, I was there, Madam. And I saw you." He studied me a moment. I wondered what he meant.

"This, this isn't the way to my house."

He nodded. "Mm-hm, I know that. Just thought you'd like a little side trip to see a view." That sounded like a surprise, so I went along, wondering if it was a wrong decision. He began a hymn that day, too. *"Once to every man and nation, comes the moment to decide."* Being partial to that tune, I joined right in. *"In the strife of truth with falsehood, For the good or evil side."* He sang the next two lines, then I joined him again. *"And the choice goes by forever Twixt that darkness and that light."* Since that day, we had only missed the one Sunday I was home with a fever.

The car gets cold. Wendall slows down and stops. "Just a minute, Caroline." He pats my knee and reaches back for a plaid woolen blanket he lays delicately over my lap. He tucks it around my legs. Things tug at me inside.

"Thank you kindly," I say. He nods and continues down the road humming a few lines of another hymn. I am warm and infinitely content with this admiring partner, who is a pure gentleman. I know where we'll go. We'll drive to the outskirts of town, then on up that steep road to the Switchback Mountain overlook. At the first bend, I can barely see the Maguire's red barn. I know the cows are looking out, waiting for the rain to stop. When we reach the top, we sit with the motor on and look out over the misty valley, the breeze blowing branches of tender new leaves. Rain begins to slap at the windows on my side of the car.

Frances Sullivan

How can I feel so happy? Why am I so delighted to be here with Wendall? He's a Northern Negro. He laughs when I drop my r's at the end of words. "Dinnah," "ovah," "mattah," he'll repeat, chuckling. My place of birth was Virginia. Everyone spoke like that. Maine people drop their r's too, in a different way.

Francis was sent to this parish in White River, Maine five months ago. The congregation acts friendly enough, but I don't feel accepted yet. I don't know where my waywardness comes from. I have never done anything close to this before. I wonder that Wendall isn't afraid for his life. But it feels like we're play-acting; like it isn't real.

The rain has let up. He rolls down his window. A sweet grass-smelling gust blows in. He raises his chin and begins a song, *"Awake, awake to love and work, The lark is in the sky;"* I sing with him, *"The fields are wet with diamond dew, the world's awake to cry Their blessings on the Lord of life, As he goes meekly by."* We both break into laughter. I love hearing his deep chuckle. He says a long, "Ahhh. It's so pretty here, and you, you are such a lovely companion." His words are a touching gift.

Wendall leans his head back on the seat and closes his eyes. His driving cap pushes forward over his eyes. I study his nose that turns up some and his clean shaven brown cheeks and chin. They look dear to me.

"Caroline," he gives my hand a soft pat. "Visions of you have begun to fill my head when we're not together. When you smile and nod in church, my heart goes tap, tap, tap." His long, brown fingers pat his waistcoat. His head rolls towards me. He takes off his cap and tosses it onto the back seat. The mass of tiny gray curls so soft, making his face seem vulnerable. I reach up and touch two fingers to the curls over his left ear. His shoulder turns towards me and his eyes catch onto mine and hold them still. He takes a deep breath. I hold mine.

Something is coming, I know. I don't want to know what.

His face nears mine. "Would you allow me to press your lips with mine, fair woman?"

His face approaches slowly, giving me time to move away. He smells of spices and mint. I sit very still and keep my eyes open. He touches my lips with his. They don't fit. They are a bit too big. But he brushes over mine softly, touches the middle with the point of his wet tongue. I jump a little. This feels mischievous. Francis never gives me his tongue. It is too personal, too secret.

Wendall moves his kiss to the corners of my mouth, then my cheeks and eyelids. My hat is knocked askew. My hands reach out to touch his waist. A momentary sideslip of his lips onto the side of my neck. A rumble rolls through me. My fingers naturally press inward. My cheeks feel hot and I am very much alive.

Then, he sits back up and looks at the roof of his car. He is still, but I hear his breathing. We are too quiet; I want to say something. I listen to the rain, and hope he will speak. He brings the long fingers of his right hand up to hold his temples, and closes his eyes. My chest feels tight. "Oh, my," he says softly. "My goodness." He stays in this position for a long time.

When his earnest brown eyes seek mine I see the melancholy ... and anguish ... tears brim up to the edge of my eyes. They do not spill. My eyes sting. Inside my breast a heavy thumping rocks my body as I try to stare away the tears.

"I'm sorry," he says looking at me again. I cannot return his gaze.

"I'm not sorry at all." My voice skips as I say this to the windshield.

He turns on the motor. It puffs warmly. As the car bumps slowly down the mountain, the sun springs out, lighting up the yellow of the trees. Long streaks of light spear through them to the wet ground.

Wendall throws me a sad smile. We pass the Maguire's red barn big stolid cow faces regard us with blinking eyes.

No. It can't be.

Wendall hums a tune. In my head, the words -- I need thee, Oh I need thee; Every hour I need thee. "No," I whisper, meaning something else. Tears steal down my cheeks.

Then, his voice wavering a little, he begins softly, "*Sing them over again to me, Wonderful words of life. Let me more of thy beauty see, Wonderful words of life.*" He looks over, nods, encouraging me to sing the chorus. His brown eyes and face are wet.

I open my mouth and try to sing along, "*Words of life and beauty, Teach me faith and duty,*" my voice cracks and I go on, just to hear our voices together. "*Beautiful words, wonderful words, Wonderful words of life;. . .*" we don't sing the repeat. Only half the words come out whole. They don't make any sense. My eyes are on Wendall. Gone is his happy countenance. His body is awkwardly stiff.

I see my house in the distance. A kind of heat wavers inside me.

His head tilts forward, like an old man. "I shall always think of you ... singing with me this way." His words end in a whisper.

I bite my lip, unable to speak. Haltingly, I make my way out of the car. I walk around to Wendall's side, trying not to look right at him.

"Thank you for the ride, Mr. Delkins."

He tips his hat, "Good morning, Mrs. Miller."

MAGNOLIA

Behold! Magnolia;
Folded bridal petals, ivory,
straining to delight.

ONE CHANCE

I was seven years old. My father had given me a dollar to buy my mom a Christmas present. On a snowy day, Mom and I went downtown to Peabody on a bus together. It was the first time I'd ever gone anywhere with her alone. She seemed very tall. She held my hand as we walked along the street and through the stores. Her pinky finger was always tucked behind my hand in a funny way. It made me want to wiggle my fingers, but I didn't dare. I was in awe of my mother. She was an adult who didn't speak to children. She never asked if we wanted anything, always assumed that what she offered would be just fine whether it was food, a game or a toy. I never felt like I had any choices.

Today, though, I was going to make a choice. The dollar bill was folded up small in my jacket pocket. When we got to the 5 and 10 Cent Store, I waited till she was out of sight, looking at mops and brooms, and went to the perfume counter. I picked out a big smoke-colored bottle with a lavender flower on it. The lady behind the counter let me smell the perfume by squirting an atomizer in the air. It smelled heavenly. She put it into a brown bag with just enough folded over at the top for me to hold onto. I gave her my dollar. She gave me a quarter and a nickel change.

I was thrilled. I actually had a secret from my mother and at the same time I knew she would be pleasantly surprised because she liked pretty smells. Would she look at me, and maybe smile and say "thank you?" She found me and we got on the bus and sat quietly all the way home. I held the bag on my lap and looked out the window to see what Mama was looking at. The bus stopped. The door squealed open. There was a little snow on the bottom step of the bus. I slipped off it and landed on my bottom. The bag hit the step as I fell. I heard the horrible sound of breaking glass; saw the wet dripping from the bag. The surprise was spoiled. I stood up holding onto the bag and crying. I looked at my mother.

She asked, "What's wrong? What was in the bag?" I didn't know if I should tell her or keep my secret still. I blubbered out that it was a present for her--some perfume. The bus drove off.

"Don't worry, it's all right," she said, and held my hand as we crossed the street to go to our house. Sniffing back my tears, I knew she wouldn't mention it again. Who could I tell how sad I felt? Maybe Daddy would be home.

I didn't get to buy my mother a present again.

She went to the hospital for surgery in April of the next year and never came home.

Portland Head Light - 1999

ISBN 1-41204035-3